PSEUDO-CITY
— D. Harlan Wilson —

RAW DOG
SCREAMING
PRESS

Pseudo-City Copyright © 2005
by D. Harlan Wilson

Published by Raw Dog Screaming Press
Hyattsville, MD

First paperback printing

Cover image: Brandon Duncan, www.corporatedemon.com
Book design: Jennifer C. Barnes

Printed in the United States of America

ISBN: 1-933293-02-0

Library of Congress Control Number: 2005902145

www.rawdogscreaming.com
www.dharlanwilson.com/pseudocity.html

For Xtine, who saved me from myself...

Acknowledgments

Acknowledgement is made to the following publications in which these stories first appeared:

"Bourgeois Man": *Prairie Dog 13*; "Cereal Killers": *The Dream People*; "Classroom Dynamics": *Albedo One*; "Dandies & Flâneurs": *The Café Irreal*; "Extermination": *Identity Theory*; "Fascists": *Milk Magazine*; "Hairware, Inc.": *Pulp Bits 2005 Anthology*; "Intermezzo": *Spreadhead*; "In the Bathroom": *Muse Apprentice Guild*; "Portrait of the Founder": *Intrigue Magazine*; "Synchronicity III": *The Wild East*; "The Kitchen": *Crown of Bones*; "The Personalities": *Red Cedar Review*; "The Rorschach-Interpreter": *Nemonymous 4*; "The Snore": *Locust Magazine*; "The Stick Figure": *The Taj Mahal Review*; "The Thumb": *Intrigue Magazine*; "When The Law Has Spoken": *Thunder Sandwich*.

"If only I could erase the future from my memory."

—John Jacob Jingleheimer Rabinowitz
(a.k.a. The Founder of Pseudofolliculitis City)

Table of Contents

Pseudofolliculitis City

Pseudofolliculitis Barbae (PB): Also referred to as "razor bumps," PB is a skin condition occurring in African-American and Irish men, and other people who grow curly, pubiclike hair on their faces. The condition is a consequence of extremely curved hair follicles growing backwards into the skin, producing inflammations, discolorations, and pusy formations. If PB is not properly negotiated, keloidal scarring can result. Keloidal scars are hard, unpleasant-looking bumps on the neck and beard region.

There are a number of procedures by which PBP (Pseudofolliculitis Barbae People) can negotiate and allay their condition. Some of these procedures include washing the face with Neutrogenie soap four times a day, shaving only once every three days, using an electric instead of a straight razor, taking two Tetracylone pills a day, applying Tendu-Wop Skin Solution, and prepping the skin of the face with a hot washcloth and Benzabling cream before each shave.

Some PBP bleed profusely when they shave with a straight razor. In many cases, each swipe of the razor produces a thick stripe of blood beads. The threshold of pain involved in this process is not great. It is perfectly bearable for those who do not suffer from hematophobia.

There are only two 100% effective cures for PB. One is to grow a beard. The other is to ignore it—to pretend that your face is affliction-free. This latter cure is of course more difficult to accomplish than the former as it requires an immensity of mindpower, not to mention that it is absurd. Nevertheless, there are documented cases in which ignoring PB has proven to be a viable cure. I happen to know a man personally who conquered PB by ignoring it.

His name is Dr. Dorian "Bling-Bling" Thunderlove a.k.a. Stanley "Third World" Ashenbach. That he lives in Pseudofolliculitis City is pure coincidence.

Pseudofolliculitis City (PC): Also referred to as "Supercalifragilistic City," PC is a metropolitan landscape of both dystopian and utopian proportions. The landscape is a consequence of centuries of industrial, technological, digital, and ultimately anal intrigue on the part of its inhabitants. If PC is not properly negotiated, psychedelic scarring can result. Psychedelic scars form on the frontal lobe of the brain and resemble the fossils of extinct insects. They have the capacity to cause a number of mental and emotional traumas, including schizophrenia, paranoia, agoraphobia, acrophobia, mulletphobia, obsessive compulsive disorder, delusions of grandeur, lack of social etiquette, lack of religious conviction, Tourette's syndrome, sadomasochism, sandwich fetishes, hat fetishes, handlebar mustache fetishes, and unmotivated hatred. The only physical effect of psychedelic scarring is pseudofolliculitis barbae. But such cases have been rare—for the most part, PB is a genetic affliction—and the fact that PB has manifested itself in PC as a result of failing to negotiate PC is, like the residency of good old "Bling-Bling/Third World," pure coincidence.

At no time should PC be mistaken as an acronym for the word Politically Correct. PC is not Politically Correct. Nor, for that matter, is it Politically Incorrect. The follicles of this place do not recognize this terminology—they don't even know what it means. They simply go about their questionable business and don't think twice about it.

There are over ten trillion follicles occupying PC at any given time. These follicles are typically referred to as PCP (Pseudofolliculitis City People). Their number is growing rapidly as far more PCP continue to be born than die in a given day. It is estimated that, by the year 12,010 ATF (According to The Founder), the population will have exceeded fifty trillion follicles. Sociologists have determined that this escalation will generate an upsurge of misogyny, alcoholism, serial killing, cereal eaters, aspiring haberdashers, waking nightmares, solipsism, megalomania, flying saucer sightings, Doo Wop zombies, Frankensteinian monsters, pheromone emissions, prosthetic genitals, haunted spacescrapers, and plaquedemics, among other things. But there is no fear that civilization will crumble like an old graham cracker somebody has stomped on with construction boots. PCP must exist in an orderly, functional society if they're going to antagonize one another in an orderly, functional manner. No matter how bushy and profuse the body of PC's follicles becomes, a meltdown will never result, because if civilization melts down, people will no longer be able to annoy, and to cheat, and to plot against, and to demolish, and to goose their fellow man with dignity, cache, and honor.

Right now, on the corner of Hamsalad Street and Blip Boulevard, a stranger has just goosed another stranger. The gooser is wearing a stovepipe hat, a black suit coat with tails, and striped skintight pants. The goosed is wearing a bowler, a collarless maitre d' jacket, and flowform slacks. When the goosed is goosed, he glances over his shoulder and politely says to the gooser, "Thank you, sir. May I have another?" The gooser nods, gives him another. The goosed nods...and backhands the gooser across the face. Now it is the gooser's turn to say, "Thank you, sir. May I have another?" The goosed nods, gives him another. The gooser nods...and then the two strangers depart and go their separate ways, never to see one another again, as if the incident had never taken place. This is a noble display of assholery. And it's not the only kind. The private and public socioeconomic matrices of PC harbor a wide variety of noble displays of assholery. They are, in fact, virtual *cirque de soleils* of noble displays of assholery.

EXHIBIT B: An organ grinder's monkey has a dream that it is the organ grinder. The experience induces a mild attack of schizophrenia. Half of the time it lacks the capacity to perceive the boundary that separates reality from fantasy. As a result, the animal often resorts to talking to itself, shitting itself, lacerating itself, eating dirt, emitting pig squeals of varying timbres, speaking with a human voice, mistaking its fingers for miniature versions of Gary Busey, and ripping the jugular veins out of random passersby. This latter affectation is especially problematic. The organ grinder must always explain to the police how his monkey had a bad dream that turned him into a virtual monster, and the police must always explain the same thing to the victim's family members, apologizing for the inconvenience and assuring them that it's a hard knock world...

EXHIBIT C: A hermit who specializes in making tall gourmet sandwiches with his feet and thinks this makes him a unique individual is deluding himself—PC is totally constituted by follicles that make sandwiches with their feet. There is not one piece of documented evidence in the archives of the PC Library of Congress stipulating that anybody has ever made a sandwich of any kind in the history of this city with anything but their feet. Were the hermit privy to such knowledge, it would devastate him; the very thought that he might be an everyman in this manner would provoke him to become a self-mutilator. But he is not privy to this knowledge. He does have chronic BO, however, and no matter how many times a day he showers and applies state-of-the-art deodorant to his armpits, he cannot rid himself of the affliction. As a result, he contemplates becoming a self-mutilator on a daily basis, scratching his chin with his index finger as he gazes out the one window in his residence at the sprawl of commerce that flows back and forth on the street in slow motion a mile and a half beneath the tip of his nose...

The aforementioned hermit lives in a $1/4$-bedroom apartment beneath a $3/4$-bedroom apartment occupied by one Mr. Krapps, a businessman of some import, but not too much import. Too much import, after all, can lead to too much ego. There is already an excess of ego in PC. So much of an excess that an immigration restriction has been placed on it. "Any attempt to smuggle, harbor, and entertain an excess of ego into this zone of existence," the restriction states, "will result in severe penalties." What exactly constitutes "an excess of ego" is subject to debate, of course, as well as what constitutes "severe penalties." It is the business of the various lapdogs and minions of The Law to determine who is guilty in this capacity and the degree to which the guilty parties should be punished for their insurrection; and in order to make assumptions about and pass judgements on so-called guilty parties, these lapdogs and minions must ironically exercise a certain amount of ego themselves. But such is the nature of The

System, and follicles like Mr. Krapps and the hermit who lives beneath him are obliged to disavow this cruel irony in the interest of maintaining a tolerable peace of mind.

Mr. Krapps' therapist is Dr. Dorian "Bling-Bling" Thunderlove a.k.a. Stanley "Third World" Ashenbach. His alias has no inherent use-value. He owns it simply because, in his words, "The more identities one constructs for oneself, the more one ceases to be One Self. And to be One Self is a dangerous thing in this schizopolis." The "Third World" that splits the alias in half is not a reference to countries that lack financial, political, social and cultural stability. It is a reference to his favorite brand of cigarettes, Third World Hellfires, which he smokes with the frequency and enthusiasm that newborn infants exercise on their mother's nipples. The "Bling-Bling" that splits his real name in half, on the other hand, is a reference to just that: Dr. Thunderlove's got the Bling-Bling as much as if not more so than the illustrious pop dragqueen diva QP (Quarter Past) Nuthin' himself.

Additionally, Dr. Thunderlove is the protagonist of this text, although he rarely makes an appearance in it. The out-of-towner might think that this precludes him from being a protagonist, the nature of protagonism being recurrent, tenacious Presence. But in spirit the doctor pervades this text, and as a result he manifests himself as the protagonist by means of his recurrent, tenacious Essence. "I aspire to redefine the nature of protagonism," he once told The Author of *Pseudo-City*. The Author's response was, "Can I bum a Hellfire?" (NOTE: Both The Author and Dr. Thunderlove are PBP. The Author's PB, however, is more pronounced: he bleeds when he shaves whereas the doctor merely gets a rash.)

Dr. Thunderlove lives in an expensive, chic-looking penthouse on the top floor of the Beerbelly Tower, which rises out of the middle of Hangtime Square. He requires most of his patients to move into the labyrinth of Beerbelly apartments beneath him, but sometimes he makes exceptions, as in the case of Mr. Krapps, who claims that he is allergic to buildings whose names begins with the letter "B." Dr. Thunderlove respects such neuroses and, being a fair man, always exempts patients that provide him with this kind of creative baloney. Except for the aforementioned, there are really not very many follicles living in PC that are worthy of attentiveness. In the grand scheme of things, they are minor details.

This is a chronicle of minor details.

PC is a subjective experience. No two follicles witness its spectacle in exactly the same way. Any attempt to perceive this place from an objective standpoint typically results in a monstrous case of diarrhea followed by an ultraviolent explosion of the eyeballs.

PC is available for purchase at most out-of-the-way convenience stores. You can usually find it hanging next to the beef jerky, which it is often confused with, both because it resembles a stick of dried-up excrement and because it has that dried-up meaty taste. Tear open the wrapper, chew it, swallow it, and in minutes your POV will be transported to an Otherworld where things aren't what they seem and yet seem what they are. But this mode of entry is restricted to tourists. The follicles of PC—they don't need jerky-in-disguise to get in here. They're born here, and they die here.

The Founder of PC was once asked if he could sum up the *Dasein* of the city in one phrase. The Founder nodded, calmly, darkly. He fingered the rim of his top hat, twirled one of the handlebars of his mustache, stroked the length of his hulking chin...

"Pseudofolliculitis City is the Chef Boyardee of Life!" he intoned, his hands proudly clenching the lapels of his skintight three-piece suit.

"Chef Boyardee!" cried the masses in dumbfounded harmony. "Who the fuck is that?"

The Founder slowly lifted up his arm. At the end of it was a shaking, white-knuckled fist. An index finger uncurled from the fist and pointed at the beating heart of the schizopolis...

...trap doors disguised as manholes swing open and suck passersby into alien dimensions...alternate realities fade in and out of con-sciousness...the Age of Immanence comes home to roost, is obliterated, comes home to roost again...gangbangers do gangsta shit and are awarded Nobel Piece-of-Ass prizes...riots and orgies break out like zits on a doomed-to-be-crater-faced teenager...a thousand sophisticated *La belle dame sans merci* grip parasols in one hand, tomahawks in the other...dandies and flâneurs leap into teeming mosh pits and are passed from Interzone to Interzone in fasttime...swooping mutant pigeons snort like bulls as they tear their human prey to shreds and viscera...pastiche of Chinatowns overlapping and cut-and-pasted together and stacked one atop the other like totem poles...orange swaths of cloud tear across the sky in fasttime all the time in the shape of shape-shifting jack-o-lanterns...zoot suits singe the streets like road runners...mad hatters bounce by on pogo sticks...sprawling electric technologies explode out of bodies and heads...sound of a happy cash register...sound of an angry driveby...sound of a background score to a blockbuster B-movie...sound of an electric violin, a maniac fortune teller, a screaming cow, a blathering Jesus freak, ten thousand road ragers, a hundred million air ragers, thunderhumming machinery, a legion of pencil-pushers blowing their noses into crinkled up pieces of construction paper, horny rednecks, rampant haberdashers, exploding piñatas, exploding pickle jars, exploding party favors, exploding pinheads...CAMERA ZOOMS IN from LONG-RANGE TELESCOPIC SHOT on the dire topography of PC to EXTREME CLOSE-UP of a thing-doer's guilty-looking bald spot...CAMERA PULLS OUT, SWINGS to one side...portrait of an in-action kung fu fight that stretches vertically and horizontally across the entirety of Little Hong Kong...CAMERA SWINGS to the other side...dark flashes of staticky figures wearing papier mâché skinsuits...sitcoms leap out of TVs sitting in store windows and attack indiscriminate streetwalkers, rendering themselves sitcons (situational confrontations)...overweight strippers with identity crises sit on café patios stuffing their screwed-up faces with key lime pie...rollercoasters full of shrieking, bearded grand-mothers thread through the schizoscape of PC in an endless spider web of adrenaline...a hundred thousand gigantic vid-billboards on which Big Brother dressed up like Neil Diamond (dressed up like Elvis) sings the refrain of "Solitary Man" with a drunken out-of-tune slur while at the same time a thousand Venus fly traps perched on window sills snap out the beat to Queen's "We Will Rock You"...a battalion of movie stars bends over and moons a battalion of papanazzis, bombarding them with a fusillade of unspeakable brown-eyes...windows open, expose atrocities, close...men in capes materialize out of thin air and go unnoticed...town criers metamorphose into Incredible Hulks and reduce entire Interzones to rubble...a lost little boy has a waking nightmare in the middle of the street and cries out for his mother, his father, his imaginary friend...vain PBP bend their heads, shield their faces...monkeys give birth to full-grown politicians and vice versa vice versa vice versa vice vice vice vice...food fights break out in sixteen delis, twelve grocery stores, and 422 butcher shops simultaneously...a mime sweats bullets as he air guitars Van Halen's "Hot for Teacher" on the corner of 7th and 2nd...a mariachi sweats banjos as he air drums Rush's "Tom Sawyer" on the corner of 103rd and 165,025th...buildings come to life and begin to digest their wretched, jobless inhabitants...a half-eaten slice of rotten spam crawls up a brick wall...a SWM (Single White Mofo) has his nose stolen right off of his face, cocks his head, shrugs and bleats, "Whatsa wigga gonna do?"...fire hydrants urinate on dogs...gators poke their nozzles out of sewers and devour dogs...dogs impersonate stray cats and are taken in by lonely women with pasty skin, beehive hairdos, arthritic fingers, liver-spotted skin, fishnet stockings, shoes with broken heels...

It should be noted that the dominant mode of currency in PC is not dollars, but doll hairs. For whatever reason, The Founder deemed the doll hair a more compelling sign of wealth than the paper bill. Originally it was the human hair, but everybody kept shaving their heads and going on reckless shopping sprees during which they would amass as much Rogain as possible so as to grow more hair and use it to buy more Rogain. It was quickly decided that this currency was bad for businesses that didn't sell Rogain (although for a time almost every business had at least a bottle or two of Rogain for sale), so it was supplanted with doll hairs, which could be more effectively regulated. The value of a doll hair depends upon what kind of doll it comes from. The lowest value doll hair, for instance, comes from the plastic head of a Britney Spears fuck doll, whereas the highest value doll hair comes from the wooden head of a Howdy Doody ventriloquist doll.

PC is of course infested with gigantic concrete doll factories.

PC is referred to as "Supercalifragilistic City" by the city's most widely read and purchased mediamag, *People!!!* None of the media-mag's editors or writers possess a knowledge of the etymology of the alias, but they do know that it is not a clipped, slightly altered version of Mary Poppins' sporty, feelgood word *supercalifrajalisticexpialido-cious*. Rather, Supercalifragilistic is a portmanteau word encompassing the words supernumerary, caliginous, fragmented, ill-natured, and ballistic—all words, not coincidentally, that might be used to describe the character of The Founder of PC, who built this place with his bare hands out of nothing more than a pissoir.

In addition to *People!!!*, PC's foremost mediamags include *The Cowshit Journal*, *The Horseshit Herald*, *The Bullshit Telegram*, *The Elephantshit Quarterly*, *The Whaleshit News*, *The Dinosaurshit Review* and *The Rabbit Pellet Press*. Virtually all of the follicles of PC read these seminal publications regularly. They also use these publications as toilet paper, a commodity that is, for unknown reasons, rapidly nearing extinction.

Sometimes the near-extinct condition of toilet paper prompts PCP to entertain the notion of suicide.

Suicide is illegal in PC. Anyone who commits suicide is swiftly reincarnated, incarcerated, and tortured for the duration of their natural life. Consequently, very few PCP attempt to take their own lives, and those that do make sure to vaporize, incinerate, or other-wise annihilate themselves in such a way that not a trace of their bodies remains.

Yesterday a man killed himself by leaping into the towering graphite volcano that rises out of one of PC's countless Interzones. He waited in line for over fifty hours before the chance to accomplish the dirty deed presented itself.

Today a man walked into a deli and robbed the place of all of its lunch meat. He also had to wait in line for over fifty hours before he had the chance to accomplish the dirty deed.

Tomorrow a man will cure his face of PB by ignoring the fact he is afflicted with PB. He will not wait in line to do this, nor will the deed he accomplishes be dirty. PB, after all, is pure and undesirable. It is one of life's many hard truths.

Hairware, Inc.

One day I woke up and decided it was time to get a job. "Jobs are delicious," I said, smacking my lips.

I rolled over and went back to sleep. Later I woke up again.

After taking a shower, bleaching my teeth, sitting on the toilet, drinking my morning coffee, eating my morning hard-boiled egg, reading an out-of-date newspaper, and allowing Good Sense to sink Its teeth into me, I realized that a job might not be the best course of action. Not a regular job anyway.

I decided to start my own business.

"Hmm," I said.

Having no business experience, I wasn't quite sure where to begin. Best sleep on it, I told myself.

I had a dream about a large room full of naked fetuses squirming on the pavement in silence...I woke up again and scrambled into the bathroom. I inspected my face in the mirror, one cheek at a time.

"Adios," I said to each of my sideburns, and then mindfully cut them off with a straight razor. I primped their bristled bodies with a fine-toothed comb, sprinkled a little aftershave on them, and tied a leash to each of their necks.

I left.

The street was full of men in capes, top hats, and Lone Ranger masks. A few of the men accidentally stomped on my sideburns as I walked them to the nearest fire hydrant. By the time I reached the fire hydrant, the sideburns were very flat-looking. I did my best to make them look presentable again.

I climbed on top of the fire hydrant. "Pets for sale," I announced. I struck a pose that conveyed an aura of relaxed confidence.

Nobody paid attention to me.

I said, "Bargain prices guaranteed."

Bodies froze, ears pricked up, irises opened...A gaggle of cape-wearers converged on me and started bidding on the sideburns. "Five doll hairs!" one of them spat. Another exclaimed, "I'll give you a hog, a cow, and two wiggers for the both of them!" Not being a big fan of the barter system, I made approving frog faces only at the men who offered me money.

I ended up letting the sideburns go for forty doll hairs apiece. The buyer wanted to pay me with an IOU. I demanded cash. He gave me 100 doll hairs and told me to keep the change.

There was no end to my excitement. A Cheshire permagrin overwhelmed my face as I raced to a bar and spent ninety doll hairs on overpriced martinis and scotches. I used what was left to buy a hot dog, a pickle, and a dirty magazine from a kiosk.

A homeless man raised an eyebrow at me as I stumbled over to his cardboard box and puked in it. I apologized and gave him an IOU for the cleaning bill.

I went back home, toppled into bed, slept, dreamt, woke up, winced at my hangover, swallowed a handful of aspirin, guzzled a gallon of tap water, went back to sleep, dreamt, woke up, stared at the ceiling, blinked, got out of bed, took a shower, bleached my teeth, sat on the toilet, ate a hard-boiled egg, read an out-of-date newspaper...

I didn't say "Adios" to my eyebrows and mustache before slicing them off.

This time I didn't even have to tantalize potential buyers with a guarantee. The moment I set foot on the street, dragging the three pieces of facial hair behind me by their respective leashes, I was besieged by whooshing capes. As I haggled and dickered and quibbled over prices, I spotted the man who had purchased my sideburns out of the corners of my eyes. He was leaning up against a lamppost across the street, petting and whispering babytalk to the hairpieces.

The mustache sold for considerably more than the eyebrows, despite the fact that all three hairpieces were more or less the same size and accompanied by sizeable handlebars...

I walked away with 350 doll hairs. Not a bad day's work. Business was really starting to take off.

I spent 300 on a prostitute and gave her a thirty-five doll hair tip. I used what was left to buy another hot dog, pickle, and dirty magazine from a kiosk.

As I lunched and read, I realized that I needed to hire somebody to manage my money; so far I had been less than frugal with my earnings. Either that, or sell enough products so as to not have to worry about how much of my earnings I spent.

"Hmm," I said.

My armpits, I thought. And my pubic region...

But I was no whore. Those hairy places were not meant to be shaved and sold as silly, loveable companions.

A nap would surely clear my mind and help me figure out what to do. I took one.

I dreamt of a room full of grouchy fetuses wearing dirty diapers and five o'clock shadows...

I woke up. An idea was sitting in the waiting room of my mind. It greeted me with a kiss, a hug, and a goose.

I waited until the sun went down and the city was crawling with shadows. I became one of these shadows.

Bums, vagrants, tramps, gypsies, hobos, nomads, vagabonds, itinerants—I started out with them. As they lay sawing logs in their respective boxes, trash cans, park benches, curbs, subway stations, alleyways, fire escapes, and roofs, I snuck up on them and relinquished their faces of any and all embellishments, which mostly consisted of unkempt unibrows and nappy, dusty beards.

A garbage bag full of booty hanging over my shoulder, I climbed down every chimney that would accommodate my creeping body. I stole a wide variety of facial hair from a wide variety of apartment owners as they snored the night away. I did this until my bag was absolutely stuffed. Then I skulked home, got drunk, went to sleep, dreamt, woke up, went back to sleep, dreamt, woke up, lay in bed, got out of bed, took a shower, bleached my teeth...

Later I set up a lemonade stand in Humbert Humbert Square.

Village idiots gathered in the Square daily to perform a *cirque d'idéotie* of feats and wonders that ranged from nude trapeze artistry to impersonations of Nascar enthusiasts to ultraviolent, gladiatorlike battle royals. It was a prime location for any business. There was always a healthy crowd of consumers looking for diversions from being oppressed by the spectacle of the village idiots' idiocy.

It was a hot day. Muggy, too. Surely consumers would be looking for something to quench their thirst.

In addition to thirst-quenchers, I sold pets.

The stand consisted of an assemblage of cardboard boxes I had stitched together with coat hangers to look like a kiosk. Over the top of the stand I painted the title of my business:

HAIRWARE, INC.

I placed a sweating, refreshing-looking pitcher of lemonade on the counter of my makeshift kiosk. I also placed a pair of sharp lambchop sideburns and a Fu Manchu there. I stroked the hairpieces with a pinky finger, combed their hides with a toothbrush...

"Pets for sale at bargain prices," I announced, tantalizing the public right off the bat.

Nobody minded me. It was the usual throng of men in capes and top hats. But there were some wearing colorful zoot and goodbody suits, and a motley few were dressed up in stonewashed Mexican tuxedos. The village idiots, if they weren't flying through the air naked as torn open clams, exhibited bright white disco outfits with giant collars that flared out over hairy, inverted chests. The idiots weren't doing anything special. Nothing out of the ordinary anyway. But clearly they had more appeal than me.

I removed ten more pets from my garbage bag and positioned them on the counter. I attached them to leashes and arranged the leashes in such a way that they were accessible to passersby who might or might not want to take them on a trial walk.

"Pets," I repeated.

Still no response. There were too many distractions. Apparently good idiocy garnered more public interest than a good commodity. The battle royal was the biggest distraction of all. It was taking place in an oversized boxing ring on the far side of the Square. Inside of the ring, village idiots were punching one another with brass knuckles, machinegunning one another with uzis, cutting off one another's heads with samurai swords. Blood and viscera erupted out of the ring in a soaking volcanic bouquet as heads bounced like basketballs into the crowd of onlookers surrounding it. I couldn't compete with the mayhem.

There was a village idiot not far from my place of business who had a zipper that ran from the top of his forehead to the butt of his chin. He was entertaining a circle of children by repeatedly opening and closing the zipper, exposing them to his grinning skull. Some of the children were crying and calling out for their mothers. Others merely stared and blinked.

I hung up a sign that read: OUT FOR LUNCH. I walked over to the village idiot, pardoned myself, glanced down at the children, smiled, grabbed the idiot by the neck, and strangled him to death. It didn't take long. The idiot didn't even put up a fight—he stood there with a bored expression on his face, waiting to turn purple and die.

Finally the bored look dissolved into a blank look, and the idiot collapsed. I turned to the children. "Well then. Wasn't that exciting? Hello. My name is Mr. Blah Blah Blah. Can I interest any of you youngsters in a pet?"

The children who had been crying and calling for their mothers began to stare and blink at me. The children who had been staring and blinking began to cry and call for their mothers.

"There there," I told them. "There there, there there..."

It was at this point that a drove of irate, bald-faced freaks stormed Humbert Humbert Square.

"Hmm," I said.

There were hundreds of them, all from different walks of life, from the highest caliber of neobourgeois yuppies to the lowliest pieces of crumpled up white trash. Spectators and village idiots alike threw their arms over their heads and emitted high-pitched shrieks as they poured into the Square like a swarm of killer bees, annihilating everyone and everything that lay in their path. A pastiche of bodies, body parts and entrails bloomed into the blue sky in slow motion...

It didn't take long for the mob to spot the objects responsible for their mania.

Since I had made their acquaintance, the hairware had been acting rather lethargic. They had in fact shown no evidence of being functional organisms. Now, however, they leapt to attention, vaulting out of the garbage bag and quickly lining up in front of me like a regiment of British soldiers. Beards and goatees filled out the front ranks while sideburns and eyebrows brought up the rear. Behind it all, mustaches flowed back and forth as if riding on horses.

The mob froze. Everybody did. Even the mangled and dismembered victims of the mob's lunacy stopped moaning and twitching and groping for their lost limbs. I cocked my head. The entire population of Humbert Humbert Square was pointing its attention in my direction.

The village idiots frowned.

The spectators stared at me indifferently.

The mob stared at me intensely.

There was a long silence during which the village idiots' frowns deepened, the spectators' blank expressions persisted, and the eyes of the mob grew wider as their chins slowly rose higher...Except for the roving mustaches, the hairware stayed in formation and didn't flinch. I calmly, repeatedly checked my watch to ensure that I would not miss taking the nap I had scheduled for later that afternoon.

"We know who you are, and we want them back," the leader of the mob finally trumpeted. He had a bald fat head to match his face and was wearing a nineteenth century Murdstone suit with a frilled white shirt, long chocolate tails, and knee-high equestrian boots. His tone was both assertive and tentative. He waited for me to say something. I checked my watch again. Gaining confidence, he shouted, "I said we want them back! Give them to us, sir! Those appendages belong to us, sir!"

The hairware began to growl. A handful of goatees barked. They had been relinquished from the faces that once bound them, yet they continued to be treated like extremities by their former masters, like parts of the faces rather than individual, capable entities. Moreover, it was obvious that they had been mistreated. Very few pieces of hairware were properly groomed, a number of sideburns had dandruff and lice, many of the mustaches had chunks of vegetable soup hidden in their bushy depths, and a few beards had been moonlighting as bird's nests...They were less than pleased. And they were clearly unwilling to return home. As pets and commodities, at least they had a chance to manifest authentic identities.

The mob could see that the hairware didn't want anything to do with them anymore. But they still felt entitled to the hairware. The leader said to me, "Call them off. Tell them to lay still. What's ours is ours. Do you think this is funny? Our faces look like baby's bottoms. Be a gentleman and return our property. Otherwise we will take them from you. You may also expect us to flog you and perform distasteful public sex acts on you. Am I clear? Do as I say."

The rest of the mob nodded at me in dark affirmation of their leader's will.

I had seen what city-goers who have had their hairware stolen could do to their peers, but I had not yet seen what the hairware itself could do. I sized up both parties, wondering whether it would be in my best interests to consent to the mob or to stand behind my product...

I said, "I don't want any trouble. I'm just a businessman. I'm only trying to make a living. There's no harm in that. I suggest you go away. Go home and grow new hairware. I can't even see fit to sell you back this batch for a bargain price in light of how poorly you treated it before I confiscated it from you. You have my answer."

There was an obscene pause...

"So be it," seethed the leader. He raised an arm over his head and discharged a shrill Indian warcry...The warcry lasted for over three minutes. The constituents of the mob stood there patiently gnashing their teeth with their fists clenched at their sides.

Shortly after the first minute of the warcry, the village idiots and spectators grew bored. If they were wounded, they went to the hospital. If they weren't wounded, they went home or to the nearest sandwich vendor.

Shortly after the second minute of the warcry, I grew bored. I also grew anxious, realizing it was time to take my nap, yet I was nowhere near a comfortable bed.

Shortly after the third minute of the warcry, the hairware grew bored.

And attacked.

The usual macabre exhibition unfolded—hot gore sprayed the ceiling of the sky like an abstract drip painting while bodies were ripped apart as if hurled *en masse* into a gigantic meat grinder. I was surprised by how swiftly and efficiently the hairware took apart their enemies.

When it was over, the hairware retreated to the garbage bag. They filed into it in organized ranks, leaving large piles of steaming carnage in their wake.

Eight-foot janitors wearing neon orange jumpsuits climbed out of manholes and solemnly began to clean up the mess with industrial brooms and waterhoses.

I sighed.

I picked up the bag, slung it over my shoulder. Saluted Humbert Humbert Square.

I walked home. Distressed. I hadn't sold a single pet. My pockets were empty. No money to buy any fun, let alone buy lunch and something to read.

Things were much simpler when I was a small businessman, I told myself. Big business is the pits.

Best sleep on it...

This time, the fetuses were in better moods. Their diapers were clean, and they had all shaved...

Synchronicity III

It was the third time I had experienced synchronicity that day.

The first time I was driving to work: I had been thinking about something and all of a sudden somebody was singing a song about that something on the radio.

The second time I was eating lunch: I had been discussing the potential existence of flying saucers with an acquaintance and all of a sudden a waiter who I had been bitching at for being too slow and too ugly threw a saucer at my head from across the room.

The third time I was walking a dog: I had stolen the dog from a bag lady and was impersonating a flâneur giving a dog a walk and all of a sudden a man impersonating a flâneur giving a dog a walk rounded a corner and headed in my direction.

I fainted. Too much synchronicity. My body lay splayed out on the sidewalk for hours. When I woke up, the bag lady was looming over me. Not only did she have an array of big pleather handbags hanging all over her shoulders, her crinkly skin was a patchwork of haphazardly sewn-together grocery bags. And she was wearing a sandwich bag over her head.

"Why did you do it?" she croaked. She held her dog's skin in one hand, its skeleton in another. After I had stolen the pet, she killed and dismembered it, unable to bear the thought that it had been in the custody of another PCP, if only for a short time. So I assumed.

"Why?" she repeated.

"Synchronicity three," I whispered.

The bag lady spit on me. She unzipped one of her bags and stuffed the dog's remains in it. She unzipped another bag, removed a live dog from it, attached it to a leash, spit on me again, and ambled away.

I lacked the strength to stand up, but I managed to flip myself over onto my side. My eyes were smeared windows. PCP in dark grey suits blurred by me. Through the blurs I could vaguely make out the flâneur-impersonator and the dog across the street. The two creatures had switched positions, and the dog was walking the man...

The Rorschach-Interpreter

The Rorschach-Interpreter was having trouble determining the meaning of an ink blot tattooed onto a nobody's face. He sat there frowning at the ink blot, one elbow relaxing on his knee, one finger furiously scratching his chin.

"Any luck?" asked the nobody. "You know, I tattooed it onto my face all by myself. It didn't even hurt very much."

The Rorschach-Interpreter smacked his lips in annoyance. "I don't care if it hurt. And it doesn't matter who tattooed it there. All that matters is what I think of it. Now for the last time, shut your fat yap and let me interpret this stupid thing."

The nobody's blank expression soured. "You're not being particularly friendly today," he bitched. "That's the third time you've been snotty with me. I think I'll leave. I think that's what I'll do." He placed his thin hands on the arms of his chair and thrust himself out of it.

The Rorschach-Interpreter kept his eyes deadlocked on the nobody's face. It was a good-looking face, despite wildly asymmetrical cheekbones and pencil thin eyebrows, and the midnight black tattoo was a splatter mark in the middle of it, tendrils reaching up onto his forehead and down onto his neck in places. It looked like somebody standing just a few feet away from the nobody had hurled a small ball of oil at his nose.

As for the meaning of the ink blot, the Rorschach-Interpreter was at a total loss. He couldn't make anything out of it.

It was unbearable.

The nobody shrugged on a trench coat and placed a derby hat on top of his balding head. The Rorschach-Interpreter flexed his jaw. He raised his hand and said, "Wait. Don't go. I'm sorry. I just have a bad case of interpreter's block and it's bugging me. I need you to stay. I need to beat this thing. Sit back down. I apologize. Sit down."

"It's too late for apologies," the nobody smiled. And pivoted on his heel. And darted out of the room.

The Rorschach-Interpreter's mouth snapped open. He couldn't believe that the nobody had run away from him. Nobody had ever run away from him before, no matter how testy he got with them. He had even gone out of his way to apologize for being testy, something he never did, and yet this nobody had still hit the road. It wouldn't do. There was an ink blot out there, an ink blot that had no meaning, that lacked interpretation. Nothing deserved to exist without having any meaning ascribed to it. Since the Rorschach-Interpreter, who had received his Ph.D. in Meaning-Making from Pseudofolliculitis State University, was the only one in Interzone 8,185 with a certificate that guaranteed he possessed the intuitive and imaginative power to ascribe meaning to ink blots, he had no choice but to pursue the nobody and convince him to stand still just long enough for his tattoo to be properly deciphered.

The Rorschach-Interpreter squirmed into a trench coat and

popped a fedora onto his head as he speedwalked out of his office and disappeared into a revolving mirrorglass door...

It was lunchtime and the streets were very busy. Stiff-backed bodies moved up and down sidewalks and slidewalks, in and out of sandwich shops and haberdasheries. Everybody was wearing a trench coat and a hat, of course. Some PCP had applied fake rubber noses and bushy press-on mustaches to their faces.

Had the Rorschach-Interpreter not been so perceptive and sharp-eyed, it would have been difficult to find the nobody.

He was standing on a corner across the street, leaning against a lamppost. He had covered his eyes with oversized Fisher Price sunglasses. In his mouth was a bite of the sandwich he was holding in his hand. He chewed the bite with a casual relish, as if he didn't want other PCP to think that he was either too excited or not excited enough about how delightful the sandwich tasted.

The Rorschach-Interpreter covertly licked his lips. He had forgotten to eat breakfast again. Watching the nobody eat his lunch was a little painful—he needed to get his hands on a sandwich quickly. But if he ducked into a sandwich shop, there was a chance the nobody would leave the corner he was loitering on before the Rorschach-Interpreter returned. He had to decide which was more important, applying meaning to the tattoo of an ink blot, or satisfying his hunger with a sandwich.

Despite the command of his empty stomach—and that was no lighthearted command—he walked to the corner and waited for the light to change so he could cross the street. There was a lot of traffic on the sidewalk. Had to be forty, fifty PCP waiting to cross. Most of these PCP were nervously smoking cigarettes and fumbling through the pockets of their trench coats, as if they were being interrogated for murder...

The nobody was on the brink of finishing his sandwich. Two more bites and the meal would be gone. The Rorschach-Interpreter tried to get the nobody's attention by flailing his arms over his head. He even called out to him. "Hey nobody!" he shouted. "You, nobody! Over here!" The nobody didn't see or hear him. Or he was ignoring him. Whatever the case, he wasn't going to get away.

The light changed.

A rabble of bodies poured onto the crosswalk. Somebody stepped on the Rorschach-Interpreter's toe, hard. He cursed. Somebody else stepped on another one of his toes, harder. He threw an elbow into the crowd, hit something that felt like steel. He stood up on his toes and emitted a high-pitched giggle, his funny bone vibrating like a divining rod that's struck water.

As his pursuer struggled to cross the road, the nobody dabbed the corners of his black mouth with an expensive-looking handkerchief, checked his watch, and casually disappeared into a nearby dimestore. Luckily the Rorschach-Interpreter saw him. And followed him.

He pushed through a revolving mirrorglass door, emerged into the dimestore. Scanned the place, his head darting in every direction.

"Can I help you, sir?" asked a security guard. He was a tall man, had to be six and a half feet, and his broad, powerful chest was grossly disproportionate to the rest of his body. At first glance he looked like a cartoon character. The effect was intensified by the fact that the security guard's head had been surgically removed and replaced with an antique minicamera. Hanging below the central lens of the mini-camera by a wire was a set of lips that resembled dried up minnows.

"Where's that damned nobody!" the Rorschach-Interpreter barked at the security guard.

The minicamera emitted a series of blips and beeps as it focused in on his face. "Calm down, sir," creaked the security guard's machinic lips, "or I'll have to remove you from this place. No shouting. No gesticulating. No making faces. No being an asshole. Understand?"

The Rorschach-Interpreter shrugged. "I guess," he said with a polite smile.

"You guess?"

"No. I'm sure. I'm sure, I guess."

"You guess you're sure?"

"Excuse me." The Rorschach-Interpreter walked back outside. He removed a plastic handlebar mustache from the pocket of his trench coat, pasted it onto his overlip. Walked back inside.

"Can I help you, sir?" asked the security guard. He knew who the Rorschach-Interpreter was. He knew he was the man who had entered the dimestore, been rude, left, put on a mustache, and come back in, posing as another man. The Rorschach-Interpreter knew the security guard knew this. But both of them pretended that they didn't. In Pseudofolliculitis City, any attempt at posing, whether it effectively dupes somebody or not, is required by The Law to be respected, to be treated as if it is real. In other words, the security guard had no choice but to pretend that this man was a different person than the one he had spoken to a moment ago. The penalty for not doing so, if caught, was to be hung naked from his toes for no less than six hours from a randomly selected lamppost and spanked with a long, half-cooked piece of linguini by a professional whipper.

At any given time, over eighty percent of Pseudofolliculitis City's lampposts are occupied by upside-down, crying, ruby-bottomed bodies...

The Rorschach-Interpreter said, "No thank you. But thanks for asking." He nodded politely at the security guard and walked on.

The dimestore was a big place. It had a high, domed, stained glass ceiling illuminated by a ring of flood lights, and its many aisles stretched out before the Rorschach-Interpreter like the rows of a corn field. Each aisle was crawling with customers. If the customers weren't creeping here or there, they were scrutinizing the dimes that were stacked on the shelves before them. This dimestore was one of the most respectable in the Interzone. PCP came from all over the city to visit and marvel at its distinctive wares.

The shelves contained nothing more than dimes, hundreds of thousands of them. There was nothing special about these dimes other than that they had all been gathered together in one place and put on sale for a reasonable price. That alone was enough to get PCP running to the place like hogs to the trough.

At the foot of aisle twelve was an olive-skinned man with a protruding, razorburned Adam's apple and what looked like a real handlebar mustache. His charcoal trenchcoat had thin silver pinstripes on it, and the face of his bowler had a symbol sewed onto it—the miniature image of a bowler. With one thumb and index finger he was holding a dime up in front of his long, pointed nose. With another thumb and index finger he was holding up a magnifying glass. He carefully moved the magnifying glass back and forth, back and forth, zooming in and out of the dime.

Unbuttoning the top of his trenchcoat, the Rorschach-Interpreter sidled up to the olive-skinned man and spoke to him out of the corner of his mouth. "Hello," he whispered. "I'm looking for a nobody with a large ink blot tattooed onto his face. He just came into the store a minute ago. Did you see him?"

Not bothering to look at the Rorschach-Interpreter, the man replied out of the corner of his mouth. He continued to inspect the dime. "I saw him, I saw him. He passed behind me and stopped approximately five feet down the aisle from this very spot to view a 1971 dime. I know the date because I had viewed that very dime myself not seven and a half minutes earlier. My mind had been wandering, I remember. I was taking note of the dime's variations, its many nuances and grooves and shiny places. At the same time I found myself wondering what the difference between a judgement and an assumption is. I don't know why I started wondering that, but I did. And I couldn't come up with an answer. At any rate, that's more information than you need." He paused. "What was your question again?"

"I didn't ask you anything," said the Rorschach-Interpreter. He had spotted the nobody walking past the end of the aisle and had no more use for the olive-skinned man, who, eighteen seconds after his interlocutor had left him alone, decided to purchase the dime between his fingers. It was a little pricey, but he liked the way FDR's dimple was abnormally deep, long, and crooked...

The Rorschach-Interpreter weaved his way down the aisle as fast as he could, careful not to bump into anybody. Judging by the number of "Oofs!" he left in his wake, he was not as careful as he could have been.

He rounded the corner, glanced left, right, left. No sign of the nobody. He stroked the ersatz hairs of his mustache.

"Ladies and gentlemen," a loudspeaker in the ceiling suddenly intoned. A few seconds of white noise followed before these words were shrieked: "Sale on aisle four! All dimes half off! First come first serve!"

The scene on the crosswalk repeated itself. It unfolded exactly as it had unfolded in the street: somebody stepped on the Rorschach-Interpreter's toe, he cursed, somebody stepped on another toe, he threw an elbow, struck his funny bone, giggled like a piglet...Then he tripped and fell on his face, crushing and ruining his fake mustache.

Once the herd had finished trampling him, he rolled over onto his back and curtly blew the mustache off of his overlip. It flew up in the air, lingered there for a moment...fell on his eyes. He twitched his face until it fell on the floor.

He stared at the ceiling.

Two feet planted themselves on either side of his head. A face moved into his line of sight, blocking his view of the ceiling.

"That looked like it hurt," said the face.

The Rorschach-Interpreter's eyes lit up. In one smooth motion, he leapt to his feet and squared off in front of the nobody. "Didn't you see me trying to get your attention across the street?" he complained.

The nobody shrugged. "I don't know. Maybe. Maybe not. I was eating something."

The Rorschach-Interpreter gave him a that-was-a-stupid-answer-to-my-question look. Then it was his turn to shrug. "Well, that's all right. I'm just glad I caught up with you. Look, I'm sorry about earlier. Really. Do you think you could give me a second chance? My interpreter's block is gone. I can feel it not being there anymore. Just stand still for a minute. I promise, it won't take any longer than one minute for me to apply at least one piece of substantive meaning to that tattoo of yours. Do we have an agreement?"

Shaking his head no, the nobody said, "I'm afraid not. The little man says no now. I can only do what the little man tells me."

Shaking his head in bewilderment, the Rorschach-Interpreter said, "I don't understand what you mean."

The nobody nodded. He lifted a finger in the air, shook it a little. Muzak started drizzling out of the ceiling's loudspeaker. The Rorschach-Interpreter cringed...

...and the nobody grabbed a strand of his tattoo, and he peeled the whole thing off like a slice of boloney he had pasted onto his face. Sound of a tomato being stepped on...

Beneath the tattoo was a hole—a hole that exposed the nobody's skull cavity, which was entirely hollowed out. Inside was a tiny little man no bigger than a human thumb. The man was wearing a wee black trenchcoat and stovepipe hat. He had been whispering something into the nobody's inner ear, his mouth shielded by a cupped palm. But once the tattoo was removed and he was revealed, he let his palm fall to his side and turned to face the Rorschach-Interpreter.

As the Rorschach-Interpreter frowned at the little man, trying to figure out if the mustache on him was real or fake, a nearby customer tripped over his own foot. He fell down in slow motion, albeit realtime returned as two pockets full of stolen goods spewed all over the formica floor of the dimestore like bullet shells discharged from a machine gun...

Portrait of the founder

So you want to know about The Founder of Pseudofolliculitis City? What in particular do you want to know about him? The Founder's attire?

A solid black ambrotype stovepipe hat with tufted forelock hanging beneath it. A classy Fairfax nipped-waisted frockcoat with puffed-up shoulders, dainty fabric tails, and tight yakskin pants. And steel-toed shitkicking cowboy boots. In addition to a giant hillock of rotting skeletons, The Founder's closet contains over 100 versions of this outfit.

The Founder's mustache?

Like his father before him, the growth is distinguished by two outlandish handlebars. It is waxed and manicured at least twice a week by the city's premier follicle-wrangler, Dr. Franklin Stashlash, a former podiatrist who was ostracized from the biz after braiding one too many miniature mustaches out of one too many tufts of toe hair.

The Founder's teeth?

White as the keys of a piano except for two dusk-colored incisors that have been replaced with the fangs of an anaconda.

The Founder's attitude?

Comparable to a movie star who has had more than his share of embarrassing run-ins with the papanazzi: polite and quiet and dignified on the outside as scenes of hideous ultraviolence flash across his mind's screen. Always makes sure to kiss little old ladies on the cheek during parades, public sporting events, television appearances and the like. Does the same to babies in strollers, albeit now and again his mental demons get the best of him and instead of kissing a baby he'll bite its head off, spit it out like a mouthful of phlegm, and start growling and posing like the Incredible Hulk. Not to worry. In Pseudofolliculitis City it is common to rejoice and throw orgies when follicles die, to cry and contemplate suicide when follicles are born.

The Founder's car?

Here is a vehicle of singular proportions, both in terms of its physical appearance and its interior machinery. This sleek-looking charcoal grey hummer limousine is available for purchase at select dealerships/rapists for a reasonably priced 98,119 doll hairs (includes automatic windows, automatic sun roof, sensurround stereo system w/cd burner, cup holder, driver's side airbag, grenade launcher, machine gun, custom pleather interior, and minibar stocked w/Johnny Walker Blue, crack pipe, and blow-up fuckdoll.)

The Founder's wife?

This Suzie-homemaker is a domestic wondergirl. Possesses a wide range of culinary talents, and prepares and serves a gourmet meal with the same pomp and circumstance that she prepares and serves a cheeseburger, fries, and soft drink. Attire usually involves some variation of conservative plaid Billingsley dress. Not too fine-looking, but not too ugly either. B-cup breasts (C-cup on a good day). Sports a tall, dry, maternal, statically electric hairdo called The Eve of St. Agnes. Takes care of The Founder's twelve children (including four bastards and one adopted Haitian) when he is "at work." For the most part the lady wears a sparkling rictus grin on her face, except late at night when she's alone and nobody's looking and she's locked in the bathroom flagellating herself with various S&M instruments. Plucks her eyebrows regularly, but not too regularly. She is available for hire at barmitzvahs and bachelor parties. Contact Barry Bungsniffer by email at theman@hubbahubbahubba.com or by phone at 555-555-555-555-555-555-555-555-555-555-555-555-555-555-555-555-555-5555.

The Founder's favorite drink?

An extra dry stirred-not-shaken Bombay Sapphire gin martini with both an olive and onion garnish poured into a tall conical crystal glass half full of ice chips.

The Founder's favorite food?

Green eggs and ham.

The Founder's favorite film?

The director's cut of Igsnay Bürdd's classic *Apocalypse Now 2: Abba vs. The East Cleveland Wiggas.*

The Founder's favorite one-liner?

"Don't hate. Appreciate."

The Founder's favorite piece of ass?

Actor/singer/writer/entrepreneur/politician/assassin/domina-trix/madame Mz. Georgiana Fiddledeedo.

The Founder's real name?

John Jacob Jingleheimer Rabinowitz.

The Founder's Existential Modus Operandi?

This is a matter of some speculation. Critics of the man have argued that his EMO is akin to Fred Nietzsche's in that he hopes to see the rise of a race of urban *übermensch* who are not subject to the vagarious moralities of mediablitzed, post-real, hypercapitalist society. Others have argued the contrary, equating his EMO with that of Stanley "Bling-Bling" Ashenbach, hyperpersonality extraordinaire whose interests lay primarily in posing for papanazzi photos, getting drunk and laid at hole-in-the-wall strip clubs, and, as his name suggests, emitting as much Bling-Bling as possible. A select few claim that he is a "good guy" who just wants follicles to be happy and live their lives according to a reasonable *carpe diem* ethic.

The Founder's vices?

In addition to gin martinis, these include (but are certainly not limited to) Montechristo cigars, Third World Hellfire cigarettes, Mz. Georgiana Fiddledeedo, psychedelic mushrooms, anal sex, painkillers, penis enlargers, shouting out swear words in church, tearing off the legs of innocent-looking insects, blackjack, poker, roulette, craps, vigilantism, gangstaism, misogyny, adultery, and every imaginable form of media technology.

The Founder's primary fear?

Waking up to a kitchen closet that has been robbed of its vast store of Count Chocula cereal.

The Founder's back hair?

Nonexistent save the odd runaway follicle on the neck region and a somewhat bushy triangular clump that his coccyx wears like a beard.

The Founder's pseudofolliculitis barbae?

Occasionally he must endure a patch or two of razor bumps on his neck region, but for the most part the affliction is under control as a result of unknown holistic measures.

The Founder's kakistocracy?

While he does not make the political scene with the gusto and fortitude that he used to, The Founder is still widely regarded as the overlord and sovereign of Pseudofolliculitis City's municipal government, despite the fact that he runs the show like the Wizard of Oz in the guise of a seedy behind-the-curtains puppetmaster, pulling the strings of this or that functionary at his leisure. As with any successful kakistocracy, only the most inadequate, idiotic, ridiculous, and evil-doing functionaries do The Founder's whimsical, absurdist deeds. The result: a city that is always-already in an invariable state of pathologically ultraviolent war and dead silent, dead still peace. A city, in other words, that is perfectly functional.

The Founder's psychological baggage?

This is also a matter of some speculation. But there are pieces of biographical information circulating amongst the throng of Pseudofolliculitis City's gossiphounds that are generally considered to be factual. For instance:

He came from the gutter, The Founder. Literally. A homeless freak gave birth to him one night as she lay passed out drunk in a sewer. The Founder slipped out of her womb, looked around, frowned, and smacked his lips. Born with a fully developed, fully functional set of choppers, he gnawed through his umbilical cord and set himself free. His mother continued to saw wet logs as the current took him away and he flowed into a drain. He lived off of sewage, excrement, and toxic waste for three days and nights before a family of mutant crocodiles found him and raised the boy as one of their own. One night, as he scavenged the subway tunnels for homeless vagrants to kill and bring back to the lair for dinner, he was apprehended by The Law and deposited in an orphanage. Shortly thereafter his family was apprehended, slaughtered, and sold to a Chinese restaurant. The Founder was five at the time, and he never got over the loss. The loss produced a series of neuroses in him (including an aversion to intimacy, unbridled air rage, solipsism, and the occasional belief that he is a swamp thing) that still plague him today, although years of therapy have allowed him to negotiate those neuroses with a certain amount of success.

Whereas the above account of the historical forces that produced The Founder as a social subject are not entirely accurate, they are by all means partially accurate, or at least they are generally perceived to be partially accurate, a fair enough thing insofar as perception and reality are interchangeable terms. At any rate, there are other accounts of The Founder's psychological baggage that are complete nonsense. For instance:

He was born with stilts attached to his feet. Stilts made of bone that were extensions of his Achilles' tendons. They were nothing but little tadpole tails of cartilage sticking out of his heels when he was born, but they grew quickly, and then they ossified into semi-straight poles. By the time he was five years old the stilts were over two feet tall. To complicate things, The Founder's mother (not a homeless freak, in fact, but a middle-class schizophrenic like his wife) enjoyed dressing him up in tall pinstripe pants, kaleidoscopic puffy shirts, spongy red noses, and glamour rock hairdos, hoping that by the time he reached adulthood clowns would make a comeback in the capitalist scheme of things and he would be prepared to excel on the job market. This unfortunate fashion statement exacerbated the number and intensity of the beatings he received from bullies of all shapes, sizes, classes, and dysfunctional family lives. One day The Founder reached his breaking point. It wasn't long before his seventh birthday. Jayke Kish had punched him in the balls during recess one day at school. The boy toppled over like a lumberjacked tree, and Jayke proceeded to stomp on his face a few times, nearly breaking his jaw. At that moment, The Founder made a partially conscious, partially instinctual and temperamental decision to do something about his degradation. A circle of laughing, pointing children had formed around his body as Jayke evil-eyed him in triumph. The Founder pushed his mangled body up into a sitting position, bore his teeth, and unleashed a tsunami of curse words the likes of which his oppressors had never heard, let alone conceived. Not knowing how to react, they stopped laughing and pointing and blinked at him silently. Once The Founder had completed his verbal onslaught, he grabbed his stilts one at a time, snapped them off of his feet, kipped into a standing position, and used the stilts like kung fu swords to beat his oppressors into bloody little pulps. He stabbed Jayke in the eye. After the incident, he was sent to a juvenile detention center and subsequently to a monastery where he was sexually abused by policemen and monks alike. The abuse produced a series of neuroses in him (including an aversion to underwear, unbridled serial killing, altruism, and the occasional belief that somebody has stolen his Adam's apple) that still exist today, and despite years of therapy he has yet to come to terms with his haywire past...

The truthlessness of such an account speaks for itself. This is one of the most popular truthless accounts of the catalysts responsible for The Founder's psychological baggage. Here is another one:

In the fifth grade he lost a spelling bee. All of the contestants had been eliminated except for The Founder and his arch-rival in verbiage, Shawn "Bring It On" Loveletter. The word was SLUBBERDEGUL-

LION (*n.* a seventeenth-century term of contempt meaning an ugly, dirtyrotten slob). The Founder was up first. He spelled it SLUB-BERDEGULLIUN, knowing he misspelled the word the moment he articulated that errant "U" but unable to do anything about it: according to the bylaws of Imago Elementary School's spelling bees, once a letter is willingly sounded off, it cannot under any circumstances be revoked. "Bring It On" quickly rattled off the correct spelling. The loss produced a series of neuroses in The Founder (including an aversion to heterosexuality, unbridled melancholy, indifferentism, and the occasional belief that he is an ocean-going pirate), despite the fact that "Bring It On" grew up to be a low-paid chauffeur for a low-grade gangsta rapper and died at the age of thirty-seven when the rapper's limo was drivebied from above by a flock of diarrhetic hawg-pigeons...

Clearly this story is full of holes, too. How would a child know how to spell SLUBBERDEGULLION, a word that is not only morphologically complex, but extinct? What elementary school upholds bylaws that deny young PCP the right to correct themselves in spelling bees? Who ever heard of a flock of hawg-pigeons killing PCP with their excrement? This is not to mention that hawg-pigeons can only be found in select alleyways on Purpuss Street, the border that divides Interzones 19,000 and 19,001, not in the monstrous suburban strip mall where The Founder's formative years took place. In truth, there are really no stories about The Founder's psychological baggage that hold water. Unfortunately we will never know who he truly is. To truly know a man, after all, is to know the degree to which he was fucked with as a child. We know he is a man. We know what he looks like. We know certain pieces of information about his body, behavior, and bad habits. We know he built Pseudofolliculitis City out of nothing more than a pissoir. We know he is over 300 years old yet maintains a forty-year-old countenance thanks to regular geriatric treatments. We know he loves his wife, but not as much as he loves the camera...Other than that, there is virtually nothing for certain we can say about the man. But as the old apothegm goes, if you can't say something truthful about somebody, open your mouth and let the horseshit fly...

For more information on The Founder, refer to his official website at www.DontHate.com. Must be eighteen years of age to enter.

The Meeting

Mr. Krapps was wearing a banana yellow tie and an angular black suit with white pinstripes. As he strode out of the conference room and skipped down a stairway onto the street, he untied and retied his tie and buttoned the two buttons on the lower half of his suit, then decided he'd rather only button one of those buttons, the top button, and he unbuttoned the lower button. Then he unbuttoned the top button, too, realizing he would rather not have any buttons buttoned on his suit at this time.

Today's final meeting had lasted a little longer than usual. Twenty-five minutes longer. Instead of an hour and a half, it went on for an hour and fifty-five minutes. The question that was addressed was the same question that was addressed at every one of these meetings: *What question will be addressed at tomorrow's meeting?* But Mr. Schmotzer and Mr. Funderburger had been in bad moods. They egregiously strayed from the question at hand, the objective of all bad moods being to create as large a community of follicles with bad moods as possible. "Why can't we discuss what question will be addressed at *the day after tomorrow's* meeting?" said the two troublemakers in snot-nosed harmony, glancing around the conference room as if baffled.

This question and others like it made for an agitating, sigh-soaked meeting. When it was finally over, Mr. Krapps was ready for a drink.

His favorite low-grade lizard lounge, The Stool Pigeon, was just a few blocks down Purpuss Street. On his way there he dropped by his favorite low-grade kiosk to buy a pack of his favorite low-grade cigarettes.

Overhead a flock of loud hawg-pigeons passed by and excreted all at once. Their manure struck the concrete just outside The Stool Pigeon as if poured out of a bucket. A sinewy streetsweeper wearing a three-piece Tenebreaux suit instantly crawled out of the gutter. He squeegeed the manure off of the sidewalk into a giant garbage bag, carefully sealed the bag, and cleaned the sidewalk with a bottle of Windex. He slithered back into the gutter.

In terms of cleanliness, Pseudofolliculitis City is an urban utopia.

The newly cleaned piece of concrete was so slick that Mr. Krapps slipped and fell on his ass when his polished Killroy dress shoes unknowingly landed on it. Everybody in the immediate vicinity instantly broke out into laughter, as if they had set him up. Embarrassed, he sat there for a moment, shaking his head, flexing his jaw, cursing the act of being alive.

As he pushed himself to his feet, the onlookers abruptly stopped laughing. They dispersed like insects...

Swearing beneath his breath, Mr. Krapps dusted himself off, combed his hair, adjusted and readjusted his tie, buttoned and unbuttoned his coat, cleared his throat, tilted up his chin, blinked, ran his tongue across his upper row of teeth, pushed out his lips, buttoned his coat, pursed his lips, removed his tie, shoved it into his pocket, unbuttoned his coat, and strode into The Stool Pigeon.

"Good evening," said a voice that sounded like it belonged to a sick duck.

Mr. Krapps glanced down at the corpse sitting in the wheelchair. One of its moldy eyes was hanging out of its socket, and its mouth was a frozen, shrieking laceration. It was wearing a brand new bowler on its head, a vintage Inkling suit on its body, and one sneaker on its foot. The other sneaker was being worn by the ventriloquist that was standing behind the corpse. There was a plastic smile on his face. He was wearing a bowler and an Inkling suit, too, only his hat was vintage and his suit was brand new. And both of his eyes were inside of his head.

"Good evening," the corpse repeated.

"Can't you be a normal doorman?" Mr. Krapps said to the ventriloquist, who insisted on using the corpse as his one and only medium of communication. In the short time he had been working here, not once had the ventriloquist spoken to him squarely; the dead, formaldehyde-filled body was always with him, and he always threw his voice into its mouth. It irked Mr. Krapps. He told the doorman so.

"You irk me."

The ventriloquist grabbed the corpse by its shoulders and pulled them up, producing a shrugging motion. "Sorry," he said through paralyzed purple lips.

"Right," snapped Mr. Krapps, and stepped inside...

Like all public places in Interzone 19,001, the inside of The Stool Pigeon resembled a conference room. In the ceiling was a modest geometry of blinking softlite panels. On the walls was a cheap brand of not-too-busy wallpaper. On the floor was a chess board of worn out carpet tiles. A vast hardwood table ran the length of the room, surrounded by a hundred or so tattered swivel-chairs. Sitting inside of a large hole in the middle of the table was the bar. The bartender was a scrawny piece of white trash wearing a barnyard tuxedo, a peach fuzz mustache, and a mullet hairdo. He had been working at the bar for over a year now, but Mr. Krapps didn't know his name. He didn't go to The Stool Pigeon to socialize. He went to drink drinks, wind down, and calmly reflect on the series of meetings he had attended throughout the course of the day.

In addition to the meeting that ruffled his feathers, he had attended four others. The questions that had been addressed at these meetings, today and every day, respectively included: *In what order will the attendants of this meeting speak today? Is the conference room we are meeting in a suitable environment for holding a meeting? What is the motive for holding a meeting? What factors determine whether or not a meeting, when all is said and done, is productive or non-productive?*

Each meeting was attended by a different group of businessmen, all of whom worked for the same firm, and none of the meetings had lasted for a longer or shorter period of time than they were scheduled to last. But there had been some interesting developments. In the first meeting, for instance, a ratty-looking insurgent named Mr. De Pood had refused to be the fourth to the last speaker, claiming that he was allergic to the number four. The arbitrator of the meeting, a shiny-scalped dignitary named Mr. Hadhair, had assured Mr. De Pood that there were twenty men in attendance and he would be the sixteenth speaker; the fact that he chose to interpret the order of speakers backwards, thus rendering him "fourth to last," was, he professed, perhaps not the most effective manner of interpretation. Mr. De Pood was unappeased, despite the unanimity with which the rest of the meeting's attendants conceded to Mr. Hadhair. He continued to rant and rave like a maniac until he passed out from an anxiety attack. The other three meetings had seen similar disruptions produced by similar imbeciles. As luck would have it, they all managed to conclude on time.

Mr. Krapps eased back into a swivel-chair in front of the bar. "Hello sir," twanged the bartender. "How are you this evening?"

Mr. Krapps smiled. "Lousy. Scotch, rocks, twist. Double."

The bartender smiled back. "Coming right up." He made the drink quickly and set it down with precision under Mr. Krapps' nose. He sniffed the drink before taking a sip, making sure the bartender had remembered his brand.

The first sip of scotch Mr. Krapps took was tiny, guarded, delicate, and stylish. He closed his eyes, swished the sip around his mouth for a second or two, swallowed it down, and released a soft, orgasmic sigh of relief.

The second sip of scotch Mr. Krapps took was giant, uninhibited, savage, and gauche. Two men sitting across the conference table glanced at him disapprovingly as he gulped down the entire drink, rocks and all, and released a dirty belch. The belch was powerful and made Mr. Krapps lightheaded, but not for long. He tapped the table with a firm finger. The bartender nodded and made him scotch #2.

It wasn't until the bartender was busy pouring him scotch #5 that Mr. Krapps noticed a disturbance at the far end of the conference table. The disturbance had been ongoing since he entered The Stool Pigeon, but he had thought nothing of it until now. At first Mr. Krapps didn't believe what he saw. He double-taked the disturbance twice, his confused frown evolving into a hard, wide-eyed stare.

"Excuse me," he said to the bartender's back, and got out of his swivel-chair.

Without moving his body, the bartender turned his head all the way around like an owl, a full 180-degrees, and replied, "OK."

Mr. Krapps looked at the bartender as if he had just pulled down his pants and mooned him. "Gross," he said. "Put your head back where it's supposed to be."

The bartender rumpled up his lips. And obeyed.

Mr. Krapps stared pointedly at the back of the bartender's head for few seconds, analyzing the sickly mullet that hung off of his lower scalp like a bushel of fish hooks. He wondered if he was just easily annoyed by PCP, or if PCP were inherently annoying. Then he got up and walked towards the end of The Stool Pigeon's vast conference table. Towards the disturbance...

A tawdry blacklight chandelier hung over the meeting, casting an eerie purple opalescence onto the meeting's attendants. There were eight of them. They were huddled around the table like card sharks, talking heatedly about something. It is illegal in Pseudofolliculitis City to hold meetings of any kind outside of the workplace. PCP that hold meetings in public establishments, if they are caught, are thrown in jail for up to 900 days, depending upon the degree of their involvement in the meeting. They are also fined up to 200,000 doll hairs and required to perform a minimum of 400 hours of community service. Mr. Krapps was a Law-abider, but he was no tattletale. Not only because tattletaling was illegal in Pseudofolliculitis City, too, but because he liked to think of himself as a strong-willed PCP. And strong-willed PCP don't snitch on their own kind. But the fact that there was a meeting taking place was not what disturbed Mr. Krapps.

What disturbed him were the ostensible mediators of the meeting.

If he was reading the social dynamics of the meeting correctly, the mediators were Mr. Schmotzer and Mr. Funderburger.

Mr. Schmotzer was shaped like a dehydrated pear. He had a thin, concave chest and wide, chubby hips that belonged to somebody's grandmother. The skin on his squat face contained patches of broken blood vessels, and on his head was a toupee that was so obviously a toupee it was difficult not to wince when you were confronted by it. Objectively speaking, Mr. Schmotzer was not pretty to look at. He was in fact disgusting. Mr. Funderburger, on the other hand, was a more appealing specimen. Mr. Krapps would not go so far as to call him good-looking, but he wasn't bad-looking. He had an ordinary physique and a full head of well-combed, dark brown hair. His eyes were too close together, like a rodent's, and his nose looked kind of like a whittled-down carrot from certain angles. But the overall structure of his face was not distasteful, and he had healthy skin.

Mr. Schmotzer and Mr. Funderburger were sitting side-by-side at the end of the table in abnormally tall swivel-chairs. The three standing, hunched-over men that flanked each of them resembled FBI agents with their sharp sunglasses, unassuming ties, and V-shaped backs. The two deviants never spoke at the same time. One of their mouths was always running, though, and a running mouth was always accompanied by a series of pained gesticulations and pointer finger thrusts, whereas the man whose mouth was closed would stare up at the standing men with eyes full of purpose and resolve.

Rather than confront Mr. Schmotzer and Mr. Funderburger outright, Mr. Krapps thought he would get a little whiff of what was being discussed. There was a vidphone on the wall near the meeting. Mr.

Krapps shielded his face as he sidled over to it and pretended to make a call. Nobody saw him.

"We see you, Mr. Krapps," said Mr. Funderburger, peeking his head over the hunched back of the man standing next to him. Apparently Mr. Krapps' stealth had not been as effective as he had hoped. Mr. Schmotzer confirmed this, adding matter of factly, "You lack stealth, sir." The two men had a nasty habit of speaking one after the other, one after the other, one after the other…

Mr. Krapps pretended he had not known the two men were there. He turned around with a surprised look on his face. "Oh! Hello gentlemen. I didn't realize you were here."

"Horseshit, Mr. Krapps," griped Mr. Schmotzer. Mr. Funderburger completed the response: "You knew it was us."

Mr. Krapps continued to play dumb. "What?" he cried, cocking his head. "That's not true. If I say I didn't realize it was you, I mean it. Why would I lie? I resent your tone, sirs. I resent you passing judgement on me with such immediacy. All I'm doing here is making an innocent phone call. Nothing more, nothing less."

"Once again," said Mr. Funderburger, folding his fingers together in front of his chin, "horseshit." Mr. Schmotzer and the men surrounding them stared blankly at Mr. Krapps and nodded solemnly.

Out of nowhere a cocktail waitress appeared in Mr. Krapps' face. They were nose to nose. She had so much makeup on, she looked like a clown. In a croaking voice, she asked Mr. Krapps if she could get him something to drink. Her breath smelled like dog food. Mr. Krapps grimaced and told her he was fine. She gave him a dirty look and staggered away. He watched her go, frowning at the heels on her shoes. The heels were almost as tall as the waitress, and she moved forward slowly, carefully, as if on a tightrope that was about to break...

"Mind your manners, Mr. Krapps," said Mr. Funderburger. "Your manners, Mr. Krapps," Mr. Schmotzer echoed.

"What did I do? I didn't do anything."

"Everybody is guilty of something," intoned Mr. Schmotzer. An abnormally large grin cut his face in half. The grin was marked by obscene calcium deposits.

Mr. Krapps rolled his eyes. This was just the kind of smart-assed stunt Mr. Schmotzer and Mr. Funderburger had pulled earlier today. He knew better than to argue with them. Best play along.

He nodded coolly. "You have a point, Mr. Schmotzer. A point that I understand, if you don't mind me saying so."

Mr. Funderburger unfolded his fingers and pounded the table with a fist. "I do mind you saying so!" Mr. Schmotzer followed the gesture by slapping the table with an open palm, then seethed, "Neither of us needs to be told when we have points. When we have points, we know that we have them. We don't need follicles bringing what we already know to our attention." The standing men continued to stare at Mr. Krapps.

Mr. Krapps stared back at them. Had there not been a handful of scotches in his belly, he might be inclined to call them out, maybe even challenge them to a duel of some kind. Despite the circumstances, however, he was feeling relatively at ease. Not that he wasn't miffed. But he didn't really care enough about his two colleagues and their minions to get sufficiently angry with them, no matter what they did. At the same time, he was interested in their meeting. What was so important that an illegal, after hours meeting was necessary? All any working follicle did day after day in the majority of Pseudofolliculitis City's Interzones was go to meetings, most of which were held simply for the sake of holding them. What kind of lunatics would want to hold a meeting that wasn't required to be held? Maybe it was because the men liked the idea of doing something so subversive. Maybe they were holding the meeting simply for the sake of holding it, only not because it was required, but because it was forbidden. That made sense. That's precisely the sort of thing two jackasses like Mr. Schmotzer and Mr. Funderburger would do. Mr. Krapps wanted to know for sure, though. He loved gossip, especially when he was drinking scotch. In another life he would have made an excellent papanazzi.

But how would he broach the subject without seeming too nosy, too flagrant? He didn't have a clue. As he had already proved, he lacked the ability to insinuate himself into somebody else's business without being caught red-handed. No reason to try and pretend otherwise now.

"What are you gentlemen discussing then?" asked Mr. Krapps squarely.

Mr. Schmotzer and Mr. Funderburger responded in harmony, and in the same square tone, as if they had been expecting the question all along. "We're talking about you, Mr. Krapps."

The expression that crawled onto Mr. Krapps face was a cross between profound confusion and outright disgust. "What? Say again? What do you mean?"

"They mean what they say," said three of the standing men, one after the other. The standing men who didn't say anything were cleaning their ears out with handkerchiefs. A squeaking noise could be heard amid The Stool Pigeon's sensurround Muzak.

Mr. Krapps bleated, "You're talking about me? You're having a meeting about me?"

Mr. Funderburger smiled, pinched his ear lobe and began to tug on it. "Yes," he said. "We're having a meeting about you."

"About you," repeated Mr. Schmotzer, and lit a long, black cigarette.

Reality slipped into slow motion as Mr. Krapps shuddered, sucked in his cheeks, pushed out his lips. Mr. Schmotzer and Mr. Funderburger waited patiently for realtime to return, using handkerchiefs to pick their noses...

Realtime returned.

"Excuse me!" cried Mr. Krapps. He stood there for a second longer and endured the stares of his antagonists before darting towards the men's room...

Inside of the men's room was a collection of men occupying themselves with the act of standing. They were all wearing tall stovepipe hats and suits with coat tails. They stood with their arms hanging at their sides, breathing and blinking in silence. Every now and then one of the men would pull out a pocket watch, flip it open, and nonchalantly check the time.

At the far end of the room was a door that led into a toilet stall. Mr. Krapps nervously weaved through the men, pardoning and excusing himself as he went.

He opened the door. He disappeared into the darkness behind it.

He locked the door behind him. He stood alone in the darkness for a few seconds. He flipped a switch.

The toilet stall wasn't very large, but it was still shaped like a conference room. The toilet was a small, low-riding conference table with a hole carved into the middle of it—more like the kind of toilet you'd find in an outhouse, only this one was squeaky clean and made out of the finest mahogany. Sitting on little stalks around the toilet were various rolls of toilet paper, some soft, some ultrasoft, some laced with aloe, some laced with vitamin E, and so on. There was no sink. Public sinks do not exist in Pseudofolliculitis City. It is required that everybody washes their hands at home and carries plenty of handiwipes and antibacterial sanitizer in their pockets. Failure to comply generally results in one of two potential punishments, depending upon the judge who sentences you: 1) you are stripped naked and tightly clingwrapped to a lamppost during lunchtime with a roll of polyethylene; 2) you are forced to eat ten deep-fried Cornish hens in one sitting. (For the record, in Interzone 19,001 it is Judge Fingerlicking who routinely ordains the latter punishment and Judge Hellonearth the former. Prior to being judges these men were, respectively, an emminent haberdasher and barber, two of Pseudofolliculitis City's most revered professions.)

Mr. Krapps pulled a handiwipe out of his pocket and nervously cleaned his hands with it. He crumpled up the handiwipe, threw it into the toilet hole, pulled out another one, cleaned his hands again, crumpled up and threw the handiwipe in the toilet hole. He stood there, not quite knowing what to do. He grabbed his chin with his thumb and forefinger, tightly, as if he feared the chin might attempt to leap off of his face if he didn't keep a grip on it. He began to pace back and forth, slowly at first, then faster and faster, until he was nearly running.

Winded, he stopped pacing. His eyebrows and underarms were sweating. He was uncomfortable. He didn't like to be uncomfortable. He needed another scotch.

He stood there.

The mirror in front of him was clean and ovular. It reflected the face of a man who has agitated insects living beneath his skin. His mouth and eye corners were particularly jittery...

There was no reason for Mr. Funderburger and Mr. Schmotzer to have a meeting about him. Meetings weren't supposed to be about follicles, whether they were perfectly legitimate meetings, or, like this one, totally illicit. And meetings certainly weren't supposed to be about individual follicles. They were supposed to be about abstractions and intangibilities and things that didn't matter. The purpose of any sound meeting was to come to terms with some form of purposelessness that was impossible to come to terms with, such as the aforementioned general interest question that was addressed at the meeting Mr. Krapps had attended with Mr. Funderburger and Mr. Schmotzer earlier that day. That was a fine topic. That was a fine issue to try and fail to come to terms with. Meetings always end in failure and a total lack of resolution. If they ended otherwise, then there would be no reason to hold them anymore.

What will be discussed at tomorrow's meeting? It was a good question. But a meeting about a single PCP? There's nothing indeterminate about PCP. PCP are as easy to come to terms with as a kick in the balls. All one needs to do is accept the fact that they are pathological and capable of anything at any given time.

Mr. Krapps slapped himself across the face to stop it from gesticulating. It was not the first time he had slapped himself across the face. It very likely wouldn't be the last.

His face stopped twitching. Mr. Krapps breathed a sigh of relief.

His face started twitching again.

Mr. Krapps opened his mouth. He let it stay open for awhile...

He closed his mouth.

And untied and retied his tie, and buttoned and unbuttoned his suit. His face was a pile of Mexican jumping beans.

What had he ever done to Mr. Funderburger and Mr. Schmotzer? Nothing. Nothing except endure their constant buffoonery, whereas most of his other colleagues had taken strides to point out the fact that the two men exhibited constant buffoonery. Maybe that was the reason they had singled him out. He was the only one who didn't come out and call a spade a spade, and he was resented for it. That was one possibility as to the impetus for the meeting. Another possibility was that his two colleagues didn't like him. Why didn't they like him? He certainly wasn't offensive-looking in any way, and for the most part he conducted himself, publicly and privately, in a non-offensive manner. Did they want him to be a more offensive follicle? Perhaps. If nothing else, offensive follicles were more interesting than follicles that keep to themselves and mind their own business. What would life be like without instigators? Boring, monotonous, gossip-free, pointless. Still, he didn't want to be the butt of instigation. It was fine if somebody else's character was being put into question, but not his. He had to find out what was going on. And he would find out. *Now...*

The door to the toilet swung open and Mr. Krapps marched back out into the men's room. He weaved through the men towards the door that led back into The Stool Pigeon.

Just a few steps away from the door, he noticed something peculiar about the men. They were still standing there like totem poles, that hadn't changed. It was something else. Initially Mr. Krapps couldn't put his finger on it, even though it was staring him in his fidgeting face. Literally staring at him.

The faces of the men in the men's room—they were not their faces. That is, the faces they had on didn't belong to them. They belonged to somebody else.

They belonged to Mr. Krapps.

There was a definite masklike quality to the faces, and you could tell they were masks if you paid enough attention to them. At first glance, though, they appeared real. The masks had the exact same contours as Mr. Krapps' face—same high forehead, same deep-set eyes, same pointed nose, same thin lips, same prominent chin. But they were made out of celluloid and colorless. And they were expressionless. And motionless.

Mr. Krapps thought he was seeing things. He was very anxious, after all, and he had been drinking.

He blinked.

He blinked again.

He blinked again.

He blinked again.

He slapped himself across the face. This time the face stopped gesticulating, but Mr. Krapps was too preoccupied to recognize and be happy about it.

He turned to the room of men, crossed his arms over his chest, and said, "What's going on here?"

All of the men simultaneously pivoted on their heels and faced Mr. Krapps. He waited for somebody to say something.

Nobody spoke.

His body began to tingle all over as his anxiety doubled in intensity. But the anxiety had made a friend now: *anger*. He had already endured a sufficient amount of oppression for one evening. Now this? It was time to take a stand.

In a shaky voice, Mr. Krapps bleated, "When I ask a question, I expect an answer. What's going on? Who do you follicles think you are? Why are you staring at me? Why are you wearing my face? I don't even know any of you. You're a bunch of strangers! Take my face off, damn you! Take it off, all of you! I don't deserve this. I won't stand for it. If this is some kind of joke, it isn't funny. If you're trying to be funny you need to try a lot harder! You gentlemen are rude. And abusive. And evil. I won't permit it. Do you hear me?"

Maybe they did, maybe they didn't. They said nothing. They did nothing. They kept on staring at him.

Mr. Krapps' tense expression curdled into an expression of pure hatred. He screamed, "Do you think you're scaring me? You're not scaring me! I'm not afraid of any of you. And if this excuse for a god-damn spectacle of antagonism continues, I won't hesitate to get physical. There are a lot more of you than there are of me, it's true, and there's not a doubt in my mind that you have the ability to collectively overpower me. But before you do, make no mistake about it, I'm going to manhandle some of you. I'm going to kick in my share of genitals before I'm beaten to a pulp, gentlemen, rest assured! What do you think about that?"

Not much, apparently—the men said nothing, did nothing, kept on staring at him...

At a loss, Mr. Krapps threw up his hands. What could he do? Despite his threat, he was not the kind of man to physically assault another man unless he was physically assaulted first. And in all like-lihood, Mr. Schmotzer and Mr. Funderburger were behind this rack-et. These men were probably in cahoots with them. Why they had chosen to express their affiliation with his colleagues in this way was as mysterious as it was ridiculous. Only his colleagues could know the truth. He had to confront them at once. Maybe there was a perfectly logical explanation for this nastiness. Maybe not. Whatever the case, Mr. Krapps would get to the bottom of it.

"I'm leaving!" he hollered. There had been a long, silent pause beforehand, and a few of the men's bodies jerked in surprise. Mr. Krapps smirked and said: "You impotent bimbos. Don't think I'll forget about this incident. You weirdos are pathetic. You may be allied with Mr. Schmotzer and Mr. Funderburger. You may be their lapdogs, for all I know. Guess what? I don't care. They're not the only men of power in this city, you oinkhogs." That said, he turned and stormed out of the men's room.

There was a narrow, green hallway that led back out to the bar. He floated down it in slow motion, peering at the walls out of the corners of his eyes...

He entered the bar.

He blinked...

Once again, he was confronted by a roomful of PCP wearing masks of his face.

These masks were different than the others. They were caricatures of his face, with bulbous foreheads, saucer-sized eyes, and chins like anvils. They seemed to be made out of some kind of tree bark, too. But there was no question that the masks were intended to represent Mr. Krapps' face, and everybody was wearing one. And everybody was staring at him. The eeriness of the scene was amplified by the fact that no Muzak was playing anymore. The Stool Pigeon was dead silent, and all eyes were fixed on a frenetic, frozen-in-his-tracks Mr. Krapps.

He scoped out the bar in its entirety. Even the bartender and the cocktail waitress had masks on. Even the doorman and his corpse had masks on.

Nobody moved. Nobody spoke.

Everybody stared.

For ten full seconds Mr. Krapps fell into a trance, his mouth half open, his eyes crossed. A tiny rivulet of drool flowed out of the corner of his mouth and down his chin...

His trance broke. He wiped the drool off his chin with the back of his hand. He cleared his throat, licked his teeth, flexed his jaw, closed his eyes, sighed...He opened his eyes and sharply pointed in the direction of Mr. Funderburger and Mr. Schmotzer with his arm. They were still sitting at the end of the bar's conference table to his immediate right.

"*You,*" he seethed, not turning to face his enemies. He kept his pointing finger on them as he glared out into space, and he spoke in a distressed yet businesslike voice. "There are a number of things I have to say to you. But I don't think I'm going to say them, because I think that the purpose of this, this—this *demonstration* is to prompt me to say these things to you, among other things. I am assuming that you are responsible for this demonstration. The reason I make this assumption is not because you are both sons of bitches, which you certainly are, but because of the fact that you were holding a meeting about me. So you say anyway. Was the point of this meeting to devise a way to annoy me, I wonder? Is this demonstration the end-product of that meeting, I wonder? Do you think this end-product is effective, I wonder? I am not asking you these questions. I am asking myself these questions. I do so because there is no point in asking you, or anybody else in this place, as I will no doubt be responded to with the same juvenile dosage of silence I received in the men's room. I expect nothing less from you follicles. You are, after all, little more than children. Only a child's demonic mind could conceive of such assholery.

68

Only a child would concoct such a scheme, a scheme whose modus operandi is evidently to alienate and estrange an innocent man for no apparent reason. As for the manner in which you have chosen to attempt to alienate and estrange me, well, what can I say? I can say this: grow up, donkeys. Halloween only comes once a year, and follicles generally stop dressing up for it when they become teenagers, unless they fail to mature in a timely fashion."

Mr. Krapps pushed back his shoulders, intensified his glare. He was carrying himself exactly as he wanted to, calm and composed yet assertive and acerbic. Nobody would get the best of him. Nobody could make him lose his cool. At this point he realized he would not find out the absolute truth about why there had been a meeting about him. Not tonight anyway. For now he would have to take comfort in his assumptions, in the judgements he had passed on the PCP that had obviously passed judgement on him.

He turned his gaze to Mr. Funderburger and Mr. Schmotzer. "Well," he smiled. "There's really nothing more to say, is there. Actually there's a great deal to say, but as I've already said, I'm not going to say a great deal, and I trust neither of you will be saying a great deal either. But I will say this: the business you've conducted here this evening has been in vain. You have not succeeded in defeating me in any way, and you never will. You have no idea how strong I am. You have no idea what I'm capable of doing, if prompted to do so. I assure you, gentlemen, this is that prompt. Be on guard. Watch your asses. We will meet again, and when you least expect it, you will be at my mercy. *That*, my friends, is a matter of fact."

A satisfied rictus grin planted itself on Mr. Krapps' face. He savored the grin for a moment, then turned and walked out of The Stool Pigeon.

Everybody calmly watched him go, following him with vigilant eyes.

Before he passed through the door, he stopped, turned to the doorman, nodded, and casually punched his corpse in the face. He didn't punch it as hard as he could, but he punched it hard enough for the corpse's head, mask and all, to snap off and topple onto the floor.

Outside, the kaleidoscope of glinting neon logos, graffiti, advids and VDT buildings that ran the length and height of Purpuss Street illuminated the night. Walking out of the dim light of The Stool Pigeon into this incandescence stung Mr. Krapps. A miasma of dark spots burst onto his screen of vision. He stopped on the sidewalk, tilted back his head. He closed and gently rubbed his eyes. When he opened his eyes, he was staring at the lattice of traffic in the flyways overhead...But there was no traffic. Not a vehicle or a jetpacker in sight. Then he realized the city had gone mute. There was no sound. No engines, no voices, no footsteps. No machinery of any kind. Even the neon lights had stopped fizzling.

Mr. Krapps dry-swallowed in anguish. "Please God, don't let it be what I think it is," he mumbled to himself, even though he only believed in God on Tuesdays, Thursdays and Sundays. He lowered his head.

As he suspected, everybody was staring at him. Pedestrians, taxi drivers, party-goers, movie-goers, nightclub bouncers, policemen, prostitutes, pimps, businessmen, street performers, bums, doo-woppers, flâneurs, dandies, street sweepers, construction workers, shit shovelers—they were all standing there staring at him, their backs straight, their feet pressed together, their arms hanging lifelessly at their sides. And there were hundreds of PCP leaning out of the vast grid of windows overhead, on either side of Purpuss Street, bearing down on Mr. Krapps with their gazes.

Their masks were something between authentic likenesses and caricatures.

Mr. Krapps was entirely without emotion. He had almost expected the spectacle. The spectacle that turned him into a spectacle...

He raised his hands in the air, nodded as if acknowledging somebody who has just done a good deed, and took a deep bow. Then he turned and paraded down the sidewalk like a king walking down a red carpet towards his throne. He walked tall, steady, and strong. He held his head high.

So high that he failed to see the wide open manhole in front of him.

He pursed his lips as he plunged into the darkness.

A gelatinous puddle of sewage broke his fall. He hit his head and was knocked out cold.

He woke up some time later. Twenty feet above him was a small iridescent circle that cast a larger iridescent circle on him like a spotlight. He couldn't see any of his surroundings, though, so he stood up and lit a book of matches.

Encircling him was a pack of alligators. They stretched out from his aching body like the spokes of a wheel and looked more like dinosaurs than alligators, they were so big. They lay there motionless, silent, watchful.

With his free hand Mr. Krapps buttoned all of the buttons on his suit. He kept them buttoned.

And said: "Nice masks."

When the matchbook died out, he laid back down in the sewage, curled up, closed his eyes, and instantly fell into a dream.

Overhead, the entire population of Interzone 19,001 doubled over as the pangs of diarrhea mysteriously set in...

The Thumb

The thumb shouldn't have been growing there. Everybody knew it. All the time streetwalkers would approach the thumb, cock their heads, put their hands on their hips, bend over, squint at it, squint at it again, and whisper to themselves: "Well then."

It had a tiny hangnail on its left flank, and its cuticle was a wild thing. The thumb's unpolished nail appeared to have been trimmed by a pair of dull, rusty scissors. There was obscene graffiti all over it, too. Dirty little words and little pictures of genitals. A manicure was badly needed here.

It was sticking out of the sidewalk on the corner of This Avenue and That Boulevard. Usually it was gangly lampposts or squat fire hydrants or unassuming street signs that rose out of the smooth pale cement of sidewalk corners, but this one was different.

The thumb wasn't tall. It wasn't short either. It stood about an inch and a half out of the cement. For the most part it didn't do much but maintain its dejected-looking slouching position. Every now and then, though, the thumb would wiggle. Sometimes it would attempt to tickle a passing foot.

PCP often talked about what may or may not be underneath the thumb. Was there a man underneath it, buried in the cement? If so, was he scared? Frantic? Deranged? Unhappy? Or altogether indifferent? But perhaps there was no man underneath the thumb at all. Perhaps the thumb was its own master. A live thumb! PCP smirked at the idea. Some of them emitted loud "Ha!" noises, while others became so angry they began to shadowbox the air in a mad panic. Occasionally the idea would prompt an angry PCP to strangle a stranger to death. A live thumb? Nobody would have it. And yet nobody ever made an effort to ascertain whether the thumb was its own entity or a mere extension of some other entity. PCP walked by the thumb, they talked about the thumb, they reacted to the thumb. But they had no interest in exposing the true identity of the thumb.

Sometimes a bead of salt water crept out of the thumb's hangnail and flowed down the length of its body...

Extermination

A slavering herd of fictional characters bumrushed a studio in which a real-TV show was being shot. These fictional characters belonged to various films and novels, both old and new, and their hogwild mission was to exterminate the real-TV characters in an attempt to re-establish the non-real medium from which they came as the world's dominant form of entertainment. They would also be exterminating the production crew (including everybody from the director down to the young male bitches who get coffee and cigarettes for VIPs), ensuring that they never produced another real-TV show again.

The mission started out smoothly enough. There were a lot of characters and crew members on the show, and it took a little while to commit genocide on them.

Holden Caulfield stabbed a cameraman in the eye with a rusty pocket knife. Captain Ahab stabbed the casting director in the gut with his peg leg. An associate producer was mangled by the sharp white teeth of a rabid Jack Torrence (à la Jack Nicholson in *The Shining*). Adolph Hitler (à la Charlie Chaplin in *The Great Dictator*) used two fingers to rip out the neck of an extra just like Dalton (à la Patrick Swayze) ripped out the neck of that no-named bad guy (à la that no-named actor) in *Road House*. Sancho Panza held down a grip while Don Quixote used a spitshined tomahawk to scalp and disembowel him. Disgusting curse words erupted out of Jay Gatsby's piehole as he caned a sound/audio technician to death. Brad Pitt's *Fight Club* doppelgänger crushed the skull of an "actor" (that is to say, a "real" PCP being played by a "real" PCP) by slamming it into his flexed, rockhard abdomen. Bartleby the Scrivener roundhoused another "actor" in the head with such power that the head of the "actor" exploded like a rotten pumpkin that's been hit by a grenade. Spider-Man and a flock of flying monkeys from The *Wizard of Oz* swooped down on a trio of gaffers, tackled them, and ate their brains. The executive director of the show was closelined by Stephen Daedelus and kicked in the balls by *Midnight Cowboy*'s Joe Buck and machinegunned by *Native Son*'s Bigger Thomas.

"Taste that you reality addict! Taste that you realtime pimp! Taste that you damned hooooooooooooooooos!" screamed a wild, bug-eyed Bigger as bullet shells poured out of the machine gun in slow motion...

And so the extermination continued, and everybody that wasn't getting tortured, mangled and murdered was having a good time. Soon all of the real-TV PCP would be on ice and celebratory cocktails and bangtails would be in order.

A few moments later, fictional characters began crawling out of real PCP's corpses.

It started with one of the victims of *The Public Enemy*'s Tom Powers. Tom stole a chainsaw and a hook from *The Texas Chainsaw Massacre*'s Leatherface. Being a child at heart, Leatherface retreated to a dark corner and started to suck his thumb. Tom called him a mama's boy. Leatherface whimpered, pouted, took off his face and stomped on it. Tom shrugged and used the man-child's hook to seize and tear out the spine of an "actor" in one swift motion. He used the chainsaw to cut the "actor" up into little pieces. "Shee what I mean? Shee what I'm talkin' about! Shee! Yeah, shee, yeah!" Tom screamed over the roar of his weapon. When he was finished, he kicked the bloody body parts of the "actor" into a pile so that none of his colleagues would slip on them.

The pile began to jiggle, to twitch. Tom attributed this aberration to postmortem muscle reflexes and set his sights on other real-TV affiliates. He didn't see the slimy, grimy hand reach out of the pile and stretch out its fingers...

The thing that emerged from the remains of the "actor" was the size and shape of a real PCP. But it was not a real PCP. Like the thing that had demolished the body it had been hiding in, it was a fictional character.

It resembled a homunculus that had just climbed out of a pool of ectoplasm. Smooth, thin, pale features dripping with junkyard innards...

Leatherface was the first one to spot it. His eyes widened in terror and he began to suck on his thumb with greater resolve.

The fictional character looked hard at Leatherface. It placed a finger on its lips and said, "Shhh."

Leatherface shrieked like an octogenarian who's stepped on a mousetrap with bare feet.

The fictional character rolled its eyes. It stuck two fingers in its mouth and whistled as loud as it could.

"Ouch!" shouted Lady Chatterly's lover. He had sensitive ears and happened to be exterminating a makeup assistant in the vicinity of the newborn fictional character when it whistled. He was in the process of torturing the assistant by pinning down her arms and type-type-typing nonexistent words onto her chest with his strong fingers. She was in agony. Her brother used to do the typewriter on her when she was a young girl, so often that it eventually induced paranoid schizophrenia in her. It took years of therapy to turn her back into a functional socialite again. But now, as the hardcore fingertips of John Thomas hammered away at her chest, The Fear was exploding back into her.

At the sound of the fictional character's whistle, however, a sickening gash burst open in the stomach of the makeup assistant. She died immediately. Out of the gash came a foot that kicked John Thomas in the nuts. He keeled over onto his side, moaning, coughing, swearing.

Another fictional character surfaced. It stood up and shrugged off the make-up assistant's skin like a Halloween costume. It was much taller and thinner than the body that used to house it, and like its precursor, it also resembled a gory homunculus.

A frowning Colonel Kurtz (the one from Joseph Conrad's *Heart of Darkness*) nudged a blinking Colonel Kurtz (the one from Francis Ford Coppola's *Apocalypse Now!*) and pointed at the newborn fictional character. "Did you see that crap?" he said out of the corner of his mouth. "That weird bastard's twice as big as that wench used to be. How'd it fit in there?"

Coppola's Kurtz didn't know what to say. He shook his bald head in disbelief, dropping the severed head of the laugh-track coordinator he had been clutching by the pony tail onto the floor.

In the half minute that followed, a raging slue of fictional characters emerged from the real-TV PCP. If the real-TV PCP had already been exterminated, the fictional characters crawled out of their remains.

If they were still alive and in the process of being exterminated, the fictional characters forced their way out of their stomachs. In some cases the real-TV PCP would simply explode, and when the smoke cleared, standing there would be a fictional character.

There were three differences between these new fictional characters and the ones that had brought them into being.

ONE: Despite slight variations in height and weight, the new fictional characters all looked the same. They had white, hairless, gleaming, sinewy bodies. Their eyes were oyster shells, and their teeth belonged to big, hungry fish.

TWO: The new fictional characters were a collection of unfamous, nameless nobodies whereas the other fictional characters couldn't walk down the street without suffering at the wanton hands of fandom.

THREE: The famous, well-known fictional characters began to wonder what distinguished a fictional from a real character—suddenly they both seemed like more or less the same thing. The unfamous, unknown fictional characters, on the other hand, didn't think twice about the nature of their existence. All they thought about was how they were going to take revenge on the fictional characters that had exterminated the meat puppets they had once inhabited.

Glass shards everywhere. Overturned furniture and movie cameras everywhere. Blood everywhere, guts everywhere.

Empty bodies everywhere. The skinsuits of what used to be real-TV PCP littered the hardwood floor like so many soaking ponchos.

Thick currents of smoke rose out of the carnage and drifted up into the rafters, into the spotlights that cast the limelights...

The smoke intensified, curdled...Suddenly the famous fictional characters were lost in a humid, gummy fog. They couldn't see anything.

Some of them tried to wave the fog away by fluttering their hands in front of their faces, but the fog only thickened. A feeling of helplessness swept them all away. It made no sense, this helplessness. Their vision was impaired, true, but that didn't merit a breakdown in their characters. But they broke down. Even the manliest of them.

"I'm scared," admitted Wesley-Snipes' Blade in a soft whisper. He wrapped his arms around his cold, leatherbound body and began to sniffle. Near Blade was Henry Miller (not the author, of course, but the protagonist of *Tropic of Cancer*). He heard the vampire killer's grief and replied, "I'm scared too, brother." The two men reached out to grasp hands. If they could have, they would have fallen into each other's arms. But no matter how hard they tried to find one another they always failed. Like all of the other famous fictional characters, they were lost and alone and feeling less fictional than they had ever felt in their lives. The way they felt—it was too palpable, too conceivable. Too *real*...

The non-famous fictional characters, in turn, were feeling perfectly fictional. They all had superhuman vision and could clearly see through the smoke. Their enemies were in pain. Their enemies were bawling like small children whose parents have abandoned them on a stranger's doorstep. And all because of a little fog. What a bunch of babies, the non-famous fictional characters said to themselves as they stood there staring at the pathetic spectacle. It made them sick to their stomachs. It made their lips curl up over their hideous teeth.

It made them exact their revenge without another moment's hesitation.

All at once, the non-famous fictional characters snuck up behind the fictional characters and used their razor sharp forefingers to unzip their backs from the top to the bottom of their spines. A communal scream of terror erupted and echoed across the vastness of the real-TV studio as the non-famous fictional characters crawled inside of the fictional characters like hungry worms burrowing into rotten apples...

Tyrone Slothrop's face turned into an electrical storm.

The body of Josef K. became a pinwheel of runaway fire hoses.

Willie Lowman's eyes lit up with white noise.

Ectoplasm leaked, sometimes spurted, out of the ears and nostrils of *The Crow*'s Eric Draven.

Max Shrek's Count Orlock grunted, urinated all over himself, and completely lost the urge to suck blood.

Reverend Dimmsdale, Guy Montag, Zorba the Greek, Roderick Usher, Rhett Butler, Victor Frankenstein, Pip, Neo, Beowulf, King Lear, Alexander de Large, Han Solo and Indiana Jones and Rick Deckard—their skin was literally crawling...

By the time the smoke had cleared, the bodies of the famous fictional characters had stopped flailing and surging. And their minds had stopped working. They belonged to the non-famous fictional characters now, and once everybody's backs had been sewn up by Dr. Zhivago, Ed Wood climbed into his high chair and said, "All right then. Take five everyone."

It was at this point that the real-TV studio was bumrushed by a slavering herd of real PCP...

Dandies & Flâneurs

A dandy grew tired of blinking. All day long, blink...blink...blink...

He bought four half-inch nails and a ball-peen hammer from a hardware store and nailed his upper eyelids to his eyebrows and his lower eyelids to his eyebags.

"That's a good idea," said another dandy when he saw the dandy who had nailed his eyelids to his face prancing down the sidewalk in his top hat, bow tie, and double-breasted twill coat. Granted, the dandy's eyes were a bit dusty and dry, but at least he didn't have to endure the tedious business of opening and closing them all the time. Better to be a little dirty and a little uncomfortable than to put forth a superfluous and unneeded quantity of effort, was his logic. So he nailed his eyelids to his face, too.

Realizing the two dandies were onto something, the rest of the dandies in the city nailed their eyelids to their face. Soon the city was teeming with dandies whose eyes were permanently open. They goose-stepped up and down the streets in legions, beaming with satisfaction.

It was not long before a flâneur got suspicious. He was loitering on a street corner in a bowler, dress tie, and quadruple-breasted frock coat when a series of wide-eyed dandies passed him by exhibiting what he perceived to be unmitigated *nouveau riche* behavior. He grabbed another flâneur by the elbow and yanked him into an alleyway. "Those dandies are trying to one-up us," he whispered in his ear. "They think they're better than us, walking around with their eyes nailed open like that. Just because they have money and we have squat doesn't mean they're special. In the end we're all a bunch of poseurs. Who do they think they are?"

"I don't know," the flâneur whispered back, peering back and forth out of the corners of his eyes at potentially threatening shadows, "but that's not the right question to ask. The right question to ask is—how are we going to react to it?"

The other flâneur placed his index finger on the dimple in his chin. "Hmm," he said. He closed his eyes and experienced a short reverie unrelated to the matter at hand. His comrade waited patiently for him to open his eyes and return to reality.

Three minutes later his eyes opened, and one of his eyebrows curled up into a horseshoe. "I'm tired of talking," he smirked. "All day long, blah...blah...blah..."

A few minutes later the flâneurs had bought their respective nails and hammers, pulled their underlips over their upperlips and nailed their upperlips into their gums. Granted, the flâneurs now owned frog faces and would have to feed intravenously, but at least they didn't have to endure the embarrassing business of being made fools out of by their fellow poseurs. Better to be a little funny-looking and a little aerated than to ignore a piece of oneupmanship, was their logic.

The rest of the flâneurs were quick to follow suit. Now the city was teeming with flâneurs whose mouths were permanently closed. They goosestepped up and down the streets in legions, beaming with pride.

As they saw it, their act of oneupmanship was far superior to their counterparts'. The only thing was, the dandies didn't nail their eyes open as an act of oneupmanship. They did it because they were lazy.

As a result, every now and then a flâneur goosestepped past a dandy and tried to mumble something. The dandy, in turn, tried to frown.

Classroom Dynamics

Situated between floors 863 and 924 of the Ameliabedelia Spacescraper are the offices and classrooms of Pseudofolliculitis State University. Roughly 200,000 students attend the university per year, and exactly 20,000 professors teach there. Most of these professors are more concerned with their scholarly output than they are with pedagogy. Most of them, in fact, could care less about their students' intellectual well-being, preoccupied as they are with churning out criticism and theory that absolutely nobody (including the professors themselves) reads and that has no bearing whatsoever on the social, political, cultural or economic condition of Pseudofolliculitis City. Fortunately, not all of the professors at PSU practice this brand of absurdity. Dr. Bobby Lee Beebody, for instance, cares so much about his students that he can barely sleep at night. He worries about their intellects. He worries about their emotional dispositions, too. The thought of one of his students being depressed or saddened depresses and saddens him. Even if they are irretrievably idiotic.

One day Dr. Beebody decided to start hugging his students hello and goodbye.

He waited for them at the door of his classroom with a friendly smile and wide open arms. As the students trickled in, he wrapped his arms around them and gave each one a warm, loving squeeze. He did the same thing after class as they trickled out. There were no sexual undertones to these hugs, and at no time did his hands slip out of place when he was hugging an attractive lady student to grab or spank a piece of ass. Not that most of his lady students would have minded. Dr. Beebody was a tall, dark, handsome drink of water who possessed an aquiline face, glinting white teeth, immaculately groomed obsidian hair, and a keen fashion sense—the complete antithesis of his PSU colleagues, who, for the most part, looked and smelled something like giant pieces of tumbleweed. Still, there were a number of his students who were less than excited about being hugged by their professor, especially the frat boys. Dr. Beebody embraced them and they stood there as if something uninvited had just been shoved up their backsides; frozen stiff, eyes wide, lips twisted, arms flush against their sides, the frat boys breathed in the scent of his stylish cologne entirely against their will. Every now and then a student would try to sneak past the professor while he was hugging somebody else, but he always managed to get his hands on the would-be escape artist. If it was before class, he would simply waltz over to the student's desk, lean down and give him his due, whispering things in his ear like "It's all right" and "I know, I know" and "Everything's going to be OK." If it was after class, he would chase the students down the hallway until he caught them. Once he chased a frat boy halfway across campus, from floor 864 to 892. When he finally caught him, he hugged him so tightly and for so long that the little bastard passed out and died in his arms. It was a devastating blow, a terrible tragedy. Dr. Beebody was just trying to be nice. The last thing he wanted to do was kill a student who didn't

85

deserve it. But accidents happen, and anyway, it is a professor's right to exterminate a student whenever he wishes. In the meantime, he would grieve the frat boy's passing and continue to administer as many hugs to his students as possible, making sure not to squeeze their fragile bodies with an excess of verve and tenderheartedness.

Killing a student is one thing. But hugging one? That's quite another. It wasn't long before Dr. Beebody found himself sitting in front of Dean Dinglewigger.

The dean exhibited the pot-bellied physique and the Old School fashion statement exhibited by all of Pseudofolliculitis City's deans. For additional effect, he had also surgically reconstructed his face in the graven image of James Dean.

The two men stared across the dean's untidy desk at each other for half a minute of silence. It was not an uncomfortable silence. It wasn't a comfortable one either. In the background, a Muzak rendition of a Daryl Hall & John Oats ballad was softly playing.

"Hello," Dr. Beebody finally said.

"Hello," Dean Dinglewigger replied. Both men spoke in dull monotones—the only way plaquedemics are allowed to speak to one another according to *The Official PSU Faculty & Administrator Rulebook*. "Personality" can only be exhibited in or near the classroom and in select public sectors.

"Stop hugging your students," said the dean pointedly.

"Why?" said Dr. Beebody.

"Do I really need to justify that question with an answer? That question doesn't deserve an answer."

"Maybe it doesn't deserve one. But it wants one. All questions want answers."

"What about rhetorical questions?"

"Them, too. They just won't admit it."

A bitter, annoyed expression tried to weasel its way onto Dean Dinglewigger's face, but he nipped it in the bud before it had a chance to flourish so as not to break The Law. "Please refrain from that sort of nonsense, professor. Please make an effort to not bring that sort of assholery to this table. Now then. You're freaking out your students. Stop hugging them. Leave them be. Don't touch them. Don't lay a finger on them. Don't even get near them. Am I being perfectly clear?"

Dr. Beebody nodded his blank face. The nod did not signify obedience. It signified a simple acknowledgment of a piece of information that had been conveyed to him. "I see," was his response. Ten seconds of dead air followed.

The professor said, "The thing is, I think my students need hugs. They don't work very hard, and most of them are complete morons. But that doesn't mean they don't need a little sensitivity and, dare I say, love. In fact, I think giving them hugs will make them more inclined to transcend their idiocy and take at least a moderate interest in cultivating their mongoloid intellects. My students need help, and I'm in a position to help them. That's the score. I've got hugs to give, Dean Dinglewigger, and I aim to give them."

The dean stared vacantly at the professor. "You're fired," he said.

"Really?" Dr. Beebody responded, as if he had just been told there was toothpaste resin on his lips.

"If you hug another student, yes, really. That's the end of this retarded conversation. Please get out of my sight. Please do that, sir."

Dr. Beebody's lips vibrated ruminatively. He nodded and said "I see" again, obediently this time. Then he puckered up his lips, widened his eyes, said "Well then," stood up, cleared his throat, glanced absent-mindedly around the office, smiled pleasantly, said "Goodbye," nodded again, and left.

Later that day, in Dr. Beebody's PB (Philosophy of the Bedroom) 310E course... "Good afternoon, studentry," announced the professor from behind his podium. He spoke in a detached voice, his chin titled up a notch. "Thank you for showing up. You may have noticed that you did not receive your usual warm greeting on your way into our classroom this afternoon. It has been brought to my attention that said warm greetings are, in so many words, neither well-received, nor productive on an emotional level. Whereas I tend to disagree with this notion, I have no choice but to respect and acknowledge it in order to avoid being skidrowed. Hence there will be no more of this touchyfeely hoo-ha. F-Y-I."

Dr. Beebody's students blinked at him. A few of the frat boys sighed in relief, albeit cagily. To sigh too conspicuously during a class was an indication of boredom, no matter what the sigh actually indicated, and if they spotted it, professors had every right to murder the guilty (or, possibly, not guilty) party in any way he or she saw fit.

"Right," said the professor. He folded his arms behind his back and walked out from behind his podium. "Right," he said again. "Well. Well then. Let's get right to it, shall we? OK then. Yesterday we were discussing the psychodynamics of Hitler's desire for his young niece to squat over and urinate on him. Let's begin today by thinking about this enchanting act of perversion in Lacanian terms. I am particularly interested in the way in which the phallus manifests itself here. Who can explain to me what constitutes the phallus according to Lacan?"

None of the students raised their hands.

"Anyone? Can anyone tell me how Lacan defines the phallus?"

The students blinked at him.

Dr. Beebody stroked his square chin. He buried his face in his hand. With his thumb and middle finger, he stroked his temples. He stroked them for over half a minute, praying to God that somebody would speak up of their own volition. Nobody did. So: "Mr. Bitchslapper? Care to fill us in?" He released his face from his hand and ogled the student.

Pendleton Bitchslapper III (a.k.a. PB3) was one of six frat boys in PB 310E. A ninth-year senior at PSU, he was president of the Phi Gamma Dipcup fraternity, the proud owner of a 0.7 grade point average, and a pothead extraordinaire; he had been high for so long, in fact, that his eyes has devolved into two small Xs that seemed to have been carved into his bloated head.

When Dr. Beebody asked his question, PB3 had of course not been listening. He had been daydreaming about having an orgy with the harem of sorority girls he kept as slaves in his bathroom closet. Dr. Beebody had to repeat himself. "Excuse me? Mr. Bitchslapper? Answer the question if you please."

PB3 snapped out of his daydream into the real world. "What question?" he asked, his X-eyes cringing like sphincters.

"Wrong answer." In one fluid motion the professor reached inside of his pitch black zoot suit, removed a large throwing star, wound it up and winged it at PB3. The weapon nailed the frat boy in the eye. The eye exploded in a gruesome potpourri of blood, brains, and bong resin. PB3 screamed uncontrollably in his seat for a moment, his body twitching and gesticulating, then abruptly clammed up and died. The killing took place in slow motion except for when the throwing star was just about to strike PB3 in the eye, at which point things slipped into ultraslow motion. After the killing, a hulking janitor in a neon orange jumpsuit crawled out of a trap door in the back of the room, picked up and stuffed PB3's corpse into a trash bag, and disappeared back into the trap door.

Dr. Beebody closed his eyes and rubbed them with his thumb and forefinger. He sighed dramatically. To say the least, he wasn't a big fan of killing his students, despite their being allergic to education. But The Law was The Law, and if a student wasn't holding up his or her end of the bargain, it was incumbent upon all PSU professors to do away with them, ideally without apprehension or remorse. Dr. Beebody almost always experienced apprehension and remorse, but he never let on to his colleagues that he did. Still, his colleagues knew he was a big softy. After all, he had murdered fewer students at PSU than any other plaqedemic in his department.

He stopped rubbing his eyes. "Right," he said. "Now then. Where were we? Yes. Lacan. The Phallus. Who has the answer? It's not a difficult question if you're willing to not be a difficult person. How does Lacan define the phallus?"

His students were stone sculptures in their seats. On average they witnessed five, six murders a day. They were no strangers to Death. But that didn't mean they wanted to be Death's friends.

Dr. Beebody cleared his throat. Nothing. He cleared it again. Nothing.

"Boy," he said. "I despise calling on people. I wish somebody would just answer the question so I don't have to call on one of you. Why won't somebody just raise their hand? That would make me happy. It might make you happy, too, if you give it a try. So. Who wants to be happy?"

No response at first. The students sat there with forearms and hands flat on their desks and eyes locked on their laps, and the professor unleashed a series of long, melodramatic sighs. Then a hand rose into the air. The hand contained long, thin fingers and belonged to Ms. Gretchen Blase, an average-looking young woman who wore average-looking outfits and hairdos and was, generally speaking, an average student. Her fingers trembled in fear as they stood up in the air. Dr. Beebody wanted to walk over to those fingers and hug them with his hand. He wanted to assure those fingers that everything would be all right if only Ms. Blase could manage to respond to the question that had been posed to the class without making a complete jackass out of herself. "Ah!" he exclaimed. "Ms. Blase! That's a good thing, raising that hand of yours. Please tell the class what's on your mind."

Ms. Blase slowly lowered her hand. She used her pinky finger to push her not unfashionable (but not entirely fashionable) spectacles up the bridge of her forgetful nose. In a voice that was not too loud yet not too soft, she said, "For Lacan, the phallus is s-s-slippery. I mean, it's not a fixed thing. I mean, it has the, uh, p-power to change. Uhm. To change by itself."

Dr. Beebody made a satisfied frog face. "Fine, Ms. Blase. That's just fine. That wasn't so hard, was it? Lacan's phallus has the power to change by itself. Yes indeed. Now that you've set the scene for us, we can begin to flesh this matter out. You're a good person, Ms. Blase. I'm not just saying that. Actually I am just saying that, because you're more than a good person. You're a great person. A spectacular person. I love you. I love you madly. And I will continue to love you until the end of time, if that's all right with you."

Ms. Blase smiled a quick, confused smile.

Throughout the class, Dr. Beebody told a number of other students he loved them. He told a few of them that he was *in* love with them. Some didn't even respond intelligently to a question; the professor just thought they looked sad, so every now and then he would point at them at random and announce, "I am in love with you, Mr. or Ms. So-and-so." And when the class was finally over, he stood by the door with his arms folded behind his back and told each individual student he loved them as they passed him by. This behavior flooded over into his other classes and lasted a good two weeks before he was sitting across a desk from the visage of James Dean again. In the background, a Muzak rendition of a Quiet Riot ballad was softly playing.

"Hello," monotoned Dr. Beebody.

"Hello," monotoned Dean Dinglewigger.

"Is everything all right?"

"No, it's not."

"Is there a problem?"

"Yes, there is."

"Really?"

"Yes, really."

"Really, you say. Well. I hope it's nothing serious. Serious problems are often problematic. I wonder what it is. Does it have anything to do with me?"

The dean glared at the professor with blank eyes. "Quit telling your students you love them, goddamn it."

"What? I don't know what you're talking about."

"Yes you do. Knock it off."

"Knock what off?"

The dean glared at him again. The professor glared back, nibbling on his lip. Finally the professor said, "Why can't I tell my students I love them? I'm just trying to make them feel good. What's the harm in that? Most of my students probably never hear anybody say they love them. Who loves people nowadays? Love is an outmoded concept. That's one of the reasons young people are such imbeciles, in my opinion. Nobody loves them. Nobody loves them, I say."

Dean Dinglewigger resisted the temptation to flex his jaw. He reached into a big tin can of lard sitting on his desk and scooped out a handful of it. As he dutifully ran it through his lustrous hair, he spoke to the professor in a perfectly candid, perfectly sedated voice. "Dr. Beebody, I hope you can hear me. It doesn't matter if anybody loves your students. What matters is that you're acting like a fucking weirdo. Students don't want their professors telling them they love them. They want their professors to treat them like the pieces of rotten meat they are. You know this, Dr. Beebody. I don't understand why you're attempting to disrupt the system. I imagine it stems from personal problems. But that's none of my concern." Having spread the handful of lard across the entirety of his hairdo, the dean removed an oversized comb from his desk drawer and began to brush his hairdo into place with long, slow strokes. "Get your shit together, sir. This is your last chance. I realize you have tenure, but as you and every other professor at PSU knows, tenure doesn't mean a goddamn thing. Its purpose isn't to provide security, it's to provide the illusion of security, and while all professors are aware of this, all professors naturally disavow it in order to maintain a relatively congenial disposition. Point of fact: if I so desire, I can dismiss you at the drop of a derby hat. You're not a bad educator. I wouldn't go so far as to call you a good one, but you're not a bad one. You need to deal with this infantile emotional crisis of yours and put it to sleep. No more hugging, no more I love yous. No more emotional outpourings of any kind." The dean paused to apply another helping of lard to his hairdo. This time he combed it in with more flair and enthusiasm. When he spoke again, however, it was in the same anesthetized tone. "Bottom line: you have issues, Dr. Beebody. Issues that need to be addressed and worked out. The best course of action you could take, in my opinion, is to go on a minor killing spree. Weed out every last sub-par student under your liege. I know there are a number of sub-par students in your classes that continue to live and breath, not to mention that you own the lowest murder rate in the department. End that, if you please. I promise you that you'll feel a little better. Additionally, it's about time you produced a piece of worthwhile writing. If I'm not mistaken, the last thing you published was some short story in some obscure magazine published by some middle-aged wacko who lives in his parent's basement. What was the name of it? It doesn't matter, it was atrocious and embarrassing. You need to write something that matters, and that isn't atrocious and embarrassing. You are, after all, a representative of this university. Start acting like one. Fiction is the stuff of village idiots. Write a piece of decent literary criticism, for once, and become a productive member of society. Do it, or get lost. What do you think?" The question was both in reference to the directive and to the glistening pompadour that was now sitting on top of Dean Dinglewigger's head like a crouching, well-groomed vulture.

Dr. Beebody blinked innocently at the hairdo. He smiled. He nodded. He smacked his lips. He said, "Well." He smacked his lips again. He nodded again. He smiled again. He blinked innocently at the hairdo again.

He rose out of his chair, cleared his throat, tipped his head, cocked his head, cracked his neck, scratched his overlip, made a shrugging gesture, freeze-framed the gesture for a good three seconds, waved his finger in the air, said "Very well," said "Goodbye then," nodded, nodded again, nodded again, and left.

Dean Dinglewigger shook his head and returned to the copy of *People!!!* magazine he had been reading before Dr. Beebody had interrupted him.

The next day, Pseudofolliculitis State University was soaked in darkness; a black cloud of towerfog had wrapped itself around the upper portion of the Ameliabedelia Spacescraper. Dr. Bobby Lee Beebody gazed listlessly out of a restroom window at the darkness, admiring the flashes of electricity that would periodically spark up. He thought he saw the visage of his frozen, screaming face in one of these electric flashes. Then he realized that he was not looking out the window, but in the mirror...

...Dr. Beebody walked down the hallway to his IS (Introduction to Scatology) 220 course in slow motion. He was wearing a pinstripe gangster suit, a fedora with a wide brim, and a plastic press-on handlebar mustache. He walked with the simulated grace and purpose of a dandy. In one hand he carried a black briefcase, in the other a black Tommy gun. The students that passed by him either made an effort not to look at him or looked at him with large, trembling eyes. The music playing in the background was a souped-up, techno version of Tom Jones' *Delilah*. It was so loud that the Ameliabedelia Spacescraper quaked from head to toe...

The scene slipped from slowtime into realtime as Dr. Beebody emerged into his classroom. As always before class began, his students were acting like a bunch of mental patients. Most of them were bitching at each other at the top of their lungs about various trivialities. A few of them were standing on top of their desks impersonating syphilitic apes. Others systematically banged their heads against the classroom's white-walls. Two took turns slapping each other across the face. When the professor walked in, however, everybody shaped up, shut up, dove into their seats, sat up, and stared straight ahead. Dr. Beebody was all business. He didn't even look at his students out of his eye corners as he goosestepped over to his podium and situated himself behind it.

"What's up his ass?" a yuppie mouthed in silence to the skaterat sitting next to him. Too scared-stiff to acknowledge him, the skaterat pretended that she didn't hear him. She pushed out her gunmetal lips and rolled her eyes to the ceiling, as if experiencing a deep thought.

The estranged yuppie mouthed, "Can you hear me?"

"I can read lips, Nancy boy," intoned Dr. Beebody, and aimed a stern, willful gaze at the troublemaker. Unlike the smaller PB 310E, IS 220 was a seminar course that accommodated 150 students and the professor knew very few of their names. He generally identified and addressed them in terms of their social image. Whenever he called on somebody to answer a question, for instance, he would point at that somebody and say things like "Can you fill us in, homeboy?" or "How about it, butch lesbian?" or "Would the piece of white trash sitting in the back row be so kind as to give us an answer?"

The classroom darkened and an unseen spotlight fell on the yuppie like an anvil from the sky. He winced. He glanced in every direction at high speed. "I'm sorry!" he exclaimed.

The professor shrugged. "It's too late for that. Die, scum." He dropped his briefcase on the floor, pointed the Tommy gun at the yuppie, and fired a round of shots in slow motion. The yuppie was shredded to pieces. So was the hillbilly sitting behind him. Blood splashed all over the students sitting in their vicinity as if thrown at them out of big pails. Sound of slung mud and choking gasps...

As the spotlight slowly grew in size until the classroom was entirely illuminated again, the janitor appeared, cleaned up the mess, disappeared.

"Oops," said Dr. Beebody in reference to the accidental murder of the hillbilly. He shrugged again. "Oh well. That's the breaks, I suppose." He carefully placed the smoking Tommy gun on top of his podium and folded his arms behind his back. At least ten of his students had hot gore dripping down their faces. A few of them dry-heaved in disgust. Some twitched psychopathically. But they all kept their composure, and they all kept their seats. "Good morning, studentry. I apologize for the seemingly off-the-cuff murders, but lately I haven't been feeling so hot. It seems that I've got a kind of a problem. The problem is, well...*you*. More specifically, the problem is that you're a bunch of retards, and I don't understand you dumbasses. That's the problem, in a nutshell. Please don't take it the wrong way. There is no doubt in my mind that each and every one of you is a worthless douche bag and always will be. But that's not to say that I don't like you all very much. I do like you, and I want you to be happy. That's all. That's all I wanted to say, for the most part. Actually I wanted to say a lot more. But what's the point? All words do is confuse people. The more words that come out of your mouth, the more you are apt to cause a miscommunication. People should stop talking to each other, I think. The world would be a much saner place to live in, I think. Well then. I guess that's all for today. Any questions?"

The professor raised an eyebrow. Most of his students stared at their laps, but some raised their hands. One student's arm writhed like an electrified snake as she went, "Me! Me! Me!"

Dr. Beebody ignored them. "OK then," he whispered. He picked the Tommy gun back up, inspected it briefly, sniffed, pursed his lips, blinked, smiled a crooked smile, blinked again, sniffed again, cleared his throat, said "Yes indeed," clicked his tongue, sighed, and fired.

...realtime slipped into slowtime slipped into fasttime slipped into slowtime slipped into...

Later, as the janitor busied himself with a mop, a waterhose, and a chainsaw, Dr. Beebody removed a pen and a piece of paper from his briefcase. He placed the paper on his podium, clicked the pen open, and stared cockeyed at the ceiling for a moment while chewing on his tongue. Then he began to write.

"The postmodern body is always-already a desiring-machine produced and controlled by the schizophrenic mediascape that encompasses it," he wrote...

In the Bathroom

I always wake up around 3 a.m., give or take a half hour. Either I'm having a bad dream that jars me awake, or I have to take a leak, or both—usually both.

There's no bathroom in my bedroom. The nearest bathroom is at the end of the long, cold hallway that cuts my living space in two. It's a crummy walk. The hardwood floor is ice on my feet, and every groggy step I take, my filled-to-the-rim bladder whines in pain. Sometimes I won't make the walk. I'll just roll out of bed and stumble over to the window and pee out of that. But I don't enjoy conducting myself like such an uncivilized Neanderthal, and I try to excrete in a dignified fashion as often as possible.

That night I had been dreaming about her again. It was a sex dream and the two of us were making love on a bed in a furniture store. A number of shoppers had gathered around the bed to take note of the love-making. All of them were wearing business suits that had been shrinkwrapped onto their wiry, metallic bodies. They were alternating between staring dumbly at us and then furiously writing notes down on small pads of expensive rice paper. I paid no attention to them. My focus was completely locked on her. On her soft, wet kisses. On her exquisite scent. On her bird-coos, her napalm sighs. On her stony voluptuousness, her hanging breasts, her aquiline face, her perfectly symmetrical, perfectly beautiful face...

I told her I loved her.

She told me that wasn't a scripted line.

I said, "I'm the screenwriter of this film. I can change the script on a dime, if I like."

She said, "Fine," and her face unzipped like a duffel bag, spilling brains and bile and bugs all over the bedsheets.

I pursed my lips.

"You're going to have to pay for that!" howled a shopper, pointing at the filthy bedsheets. But he was not a shopper at all. He was the mayor of the furniture store, and his decree was more than I could bear...

I snapped awake. My groin felt like it was on fire. Screw civility. I had to go too badly to make it to the bathroom anyway. I rolled out of bed. In two quick strides I was standing in front of the window, nude, in pain, traces of my dream slithering through the loopholes of my consciousness.

I couldn't get the window open.

It was stuck.

Stuck!

The latch wouldn't turn. It had rusted over. When was the last time I opened the window? The last time I peed out the window. When was that? Couldn't remember, couldn't remember. A long time ago? Maybe. Maybe not. Whatever the case, the goddamn latch wouldn't budge. But I kept at it, and I depleted the store of dirty words in my lexicon two times over, starting slowly and softly at first, then picking up speed and sound. Then swearing like a motherfucking flamethrower. I considered smashing the window. At the last second I managed to control myself. I would use the bathroom like a normal, grown up person, no matter how badly I had to go. I just had to get there *fast*.

I stopped swearing. I strode out of my bedroom.

I ran into a line. The back of one. There was a line of follicles here, and it ran the length of my hallway.

My hand was firmly gripping my crotch, my knees were bent, my feet were pigeon-toed, my face was all scrunched up. "What is this?" I said. Nobody answered me. Nobody even turned around to scowl at me.

The line consisted of about twenty men. They all wore business suits that were far too large for their bodies. They looked like children dressed up in their parents' clothes.

"I *said*," I carped, "what the hell is this!" This time a few men turned and looked over their shoulders. One responded to me with a shrug. But nobody said anything.

Irate, I started walking towards the bathroom. My hand remained attached to my crotch. Not because I was naked—I could've cared less about that. At this point, if I removed my hand, it would be like removing the cap from a shaken up bottle of beer. I tried to walk tall and powerfully, but it was difficult; my bladder demanded that I bend my head and body.

"No cutting," said the man at the end of the line as I brushed past him. "He's cutting. Look, fellas. Somebody thinks he can get away with something."

"I'm not trying to get away with anything!" I shouted, continuing to move forward. "This is my place and I can do whatever I want to—"

A hard, rigid arm snapped up in front of me. Its elbow was in line with my Adam's apple and I clotheslined myself against it. My feet and legs flew out from under me and headed for the ceiling. The wind was knocked out of me as my shoulderblades slammed into the floor. My hand came loose from my crotch. I expected to wet myself, but I didn't. Apparently I had more self-control than I gave myself credit for. Still, my pee pangs were excruciating, more so now that I was gasping and dry-heaving, trying to get my wind back.

It was a good half a minute before I was able to breathe normally again. I blundered to my feet and faced the man who had stuck his arm out. He didn't face me. He continued to stare at the back of the man's head in front of him. His nose and chin were sharper than Ginsu knives, and his tight lips twitched in distress, as if he was trying to keep something from squeezing its way out of his mouth.

"I know what you did," I said matter of factly, "and I'm not very happy about it. You could've killed me. Not to mention that you almost made me piss myself. What's your problem? What're you doing here anyway? I'm talking to you."

His lips twitched with more resolve, but he didn't say anything. I took a step closer and stared at him as hard as I possibly could. It was a little chilly out here and my body wanted to shiver. I didn't let it.

"No cutting," the man finally uttered. "Those are the rules."

I made a face. "The rules? What is this, preschool? Do the rules say anything about breaking and entering?"

The man frowned, not knowing how to answer the question.

I rolled my eyes. Patience was not a luxury I could afford.

I backstepped across the hallway until I hit the wall.

I took a deep breath, held it in for a few seconds...and addressed the entire line. "Intruders, listen up!" It hurt down low to yell like that.

I reapplied my hand to my genitals and lowered my voice a notch. "Listen up, I said! I don't know where you sons of bitches came from or what you think you're doing! And I don't care! Not right now! I need to use that goddamn toilet! It's my toilet! None of this no cutting bullshit! Understand? Fine!" Without hesitation, I started for the bathroom again.

It was easier to get there than I expected. Some of the men said a few derogatory things out of the corners of their mouths as I passed them, and a few poked me with their thumbs, but with very little determination: all they succeeded in doing was making me giggle and exacerbating the condition of my bladder. For the most part they seemed reluctant to step out of line. Maybe they were worried they would lose their position and be sent to the back? Maybe they had orders to stay in place, or else? Or else what? Who was giving the orders? Who was making "the rules"? And why?...None of it mattered. I'd get to the bottom of this nonsense later. Right now I had business to attend to, and it would take a lot more than a bunch of meek, insufficiently dressed follicles to stop me from attending to it.

At last I made it to the front of the line. The door to the bathroom was closed. The first man in line had his nose pressed up against it.

"Get your nose off of my door," I said.

He didn't obey.

I smiled, nodded. Cleared my throat.

I swung my free arm around and pounded on the door as hard as I could, once, with my fist. The blow caused the door to reverberate and punch the man in the face. A chain reaction resulted. His head snapped back and hit the head of the man behind him, and that man's head snapped back and hit the man behind him, and that man's head hit the next man's head, and so on, and so on, all the way down the line. To initiate this domino effect wasn't my intent. Still, it gave me a great deal of pleasure, watching them all clutch their noses in pain.

"Maybe that'll teach you weird bastards not to invade a man's privacy," I announced, and focused my attention on the man in front of the door.

"Who's in there?"

No response. Unlike the face of the man in the back of the line, this one's was round and pudgy. And his brow was abnormally distended.

"I said who's in there? Look at me when I'm talking to you."

He didn't look at me. He massaged his hurt nose, delicately, with a thumb and index finger. His gaze remained firmly affixed to the door.

"Answer my question. Answer my question. Answer my question."

The man stopped massaging his nose. He let his arm fall back down to his side. I widened my eyes, bore my teeth. The man squeaked, "No...cutting." He looked like he was on the brink of tears.

I lit a fire on his face with a quick backhand. "What's that you said?"

His eyes blinked erratically and his lips experienced a series of heinous spasms. No looking at me, though. No speaking to me either.

That did it. "Out of my way!" I exclaimed, and battle-rammed the man with one of my shoulders, sending him smack into the wall on the far side of the hallway. He hit his head and slid to the floor, knocked out cold. The eyes of the man behind him bulged in astonishment, but he didn't do anything. Nobody did anything.

Big surprise.

I took the man's place in front of the door and began hammering on it. "Open up! Open up! I hafta use that toilet RIGHT NOW! Get outta my bathroom! Get out! Get out! Get out! Get out!" As I

104

screamed, my pee pangs thunder-echoed inside of my body.

I heard some rustling behind the door. And some hurried, muffled whispering. But the door stayed closed. I wanted to bash it in. Now, though, the effort would definitely cause me to spring a storming leak, no matter how hard I continued to squeeze myself. And doors are expensive, one of Pseudofolliculitis City's hottest commodities alongside sandwiches and hats. I couldn't afford to buy another one. What could I do?

It dawned on me that the door might not be locked. There was no reason why it shouldn't have been locked. Any reasonable person that sees a line of people strung out in front of a door would draw the conclusion that it was locked; if it wasn't, what was to prohibit the entire line from systematically piling into the space that existed on the other side of the door? Still, this line wasn't like other lines. This line was a crock of shit. Reason would dictate that the door was locked, but reason was not something that could be applied to this situation. Therefore the door was unlocked? No, that would be a reasonable deduction based on the application of reason to an anti-reasonable event. But that didn't mean the door wasn't unlocked. It could have been locked or unlocked—there was no way to dialectically determine whether it was one or the other without trying it.

I gripped the knob, turned it, pushed on it.

The door opened.

A goofy smile landed on my face like an exclamation point. I pushed the door all the way open and stepped into the bathroom, anticipating the ecstatic relief I would feel in just a few short seconds...

I froze. Reality skipped a beat, and my eyebrows began sweating.

It was her. I couldn't see her. But I knew it was her.

She was wearing a yak costume. Like the men's suits, the costume was too big for her—it's skin hung from her body like wet construction paper. The skin seemed to have been recently peeled off the yak it used to belong to. It was covered with patches of dark, gleaming blood. In places the blood was dripping off of her. Every time a drop struck the floor, it splashed and bloomed in slowtime...The head of the yak was a caricature. Its sharp horns were too long and thick, its dilated eyes were too round and wide. And its mouth was far too small to contain the hulking set of teeth that was inside of it. At any moment, the teeth seemed as if they might snap backwards like a bear trap and devour the monstrous head.

I tried to shout something. All that came out of my mouth was a creaking whisper...

He was standing in front of the toilet. He had a mustache that appeared to have been painted onto his face. I double-taked the mustache and realized that it was the other way around: the face had been painted behind the mustache...

A long, hard penis was sticking out of his pants.

She was kneeling down in front of him, tightly gripping the shaft of his penis in one of her elastic hooves. In her other hoof was a large magic marker she used to draw a smiley face onto the head of the penis.

When she was finished, she removed a small rectangular cage from a pouch in her stomach. The cage had a small hole in one end. She unlocked it, unfolded it, snapped it onto the man's penis, and locked it. "Only the caged bird can sing," she said.

The man nodded grimly.

He thanked her, bowed to her. He carefully inserted his prisoner into his baggy pants.

He excused himself as he ambled passed me, his murky face reeking of wet paint. The window on the other side of the bathroom was open. He crawled out of it, tumbled down and fell off of the roof.

I swallowed a mouthful of sand...

She stood up. She put her front two hooves on her hips and stared at me. I stared back at her, hunched over, frog-faced, my hand still married to my crotch.

I whispered, "I have to use the toilet."

"Next!" she blurted in an annoyed, Old Maid's voice. Another man, the one I had knocked out, stepped into the bathroom and mindfully closed the door behind him.

Paying no attention to me, he took his spot in front of the toilet, unzipped his pants, and removed his penis. She knelt down, grabbed the penis, stroked it until it was hard, and gave it a personality...

Dazed, I glanced at myself in the mirror hanging over the bathroom sink. My reflection blinked at me. Or winked at me. I wasn't sure which.

As I emptied my bladder into the sink, moaning and groaning in pleasure, I watched them out of the corners of my eyes. My vision was failing me. The power of sight seemed to be leaking out of my bladder. But I could still see her teeth. I could see the man's pinched-together eyes, too, and when she caged his bird, I could hear him moaning and groaning in pleasure...

The Widow's Peaks

The thing-doer couldn't stop staring at his widow's peaks in the mirror. He wanted to stop staring at them, but it was impossible. They were creeping backwards across his scalp! Soon he would be bald. His widow's peaks would cease to be widow's peaks; they would merge into one smooth entity and render his scalp a desert of vast eternity...The thing-doer vowed to appreciate his widow's peaks while they still existed. Every morning he got out of bed and did his morning things, then turned to his mirror and proceeded to stare at himself until the evening, at which point he would do his evening things and finally go back to bed.

One morning the thing-doer was in the middle of doing his morning things when he experienced a funny, tickling sensation on his upper forehead. Fearing the worst, he quickly spit his breakfast out of his mouth and hurried over to his mirror.

He didn't believe what he saw at first. After a certain amount of deranged scrutiny, however, he had no choice but to believe it: the widow's peaks, the two pizza slices of baldness that had once characterized his hairline, were gone. His hairline was no longer the eroding, weak-looking piece of real estate it used to be. Now it was as strong and straight across as it had been when he was a teenager. The thing-doer's face lit up with glee, and he chirped like a bird despite the fact that he was a heavily medicated manic depressive and wasn't supposed to bird-chirp with glee under any circumstances, doctor's orders. Not to worry. Just as quickly as the good mood overcame him, it faded away, and his monobrow collapsed into a suspicious, distressed V.

Where had the widow's peaks gone? They didn't just disappear into thin air. Widow's peaks don't do things like that.

A rustling noise was being made in his bedroom. Probably just a thief. But maybe not, maybe not...

"Hello?" the thing-doer said, turning and looking over his shoulder. "Is anybody there?"

No response.

"If you're robbing me, tell me. I don't mind. I get robbed all the time. It's fun."

No response.

"I'm serious. I'll even help you find some things to steal. I'll whip you up a snack, too. I make a mean finger sandwich. Hello?"

Again, a rustling noise...

The thing-doer loaded his .44 magnum and prowled down the hallway towards his bedroom. He hesitated in front of the bedroom door, listening, listening...The door was open a crack but he couldn't see anything through it. Taking a deep breath, he placed a fingertip on the door and slowly pushed it open.

He cocked the gun and said, "Freeze." The tone of the spoken word was somewhere between a command and a question.

The widow's peaks froze. Not because they had been told to freeze, but because they had been startled. They were in the process of putting on the thing-doer's favorite pinstripe suit. Their motive for doing so, he surmised, was to wear it.

Once the widow's peaks realized that it was only their former possessor who had startled them, they sort of huffed, as if the idea of the thing-doer being any kind of threat to them was absurd, gun in hand or not. The thing-doer sensed the meaning of the huff, but he didn't say anything about it. Instead he said, "I don't think I like what I'm seeing."

The widow's peaks shrugged. They tightened his tie, zipped up his pants, adjusted his cuff links.

They nodded.

The thing-doer widened his eyes, shook his head.

The widow's peaks took three manly strides across the bedroom and dove out an open window. The thing-doer tried to grab them. He missed.

The widow's peaks fell 100 flights onto a busy sidewalk. They landed on a loiterer's head. Luckily they didn't weigh that much, and after the loiterer finished kicking and stomping on them, they got up, dusted themselves off, and calmly walked away.

"You defenestrating bastards!" hollered the thing-doer, hanging out the window and shaking his fist. "You stole my suit! Hey! I'm talking to you!"

The jetpackers in the flyway outside of the window came to a sharp halt. All of them were wearing sharp-edged pseudosuits. Hovering there, they glanced at the thing-doer with offended, hateful expressions on their faces.

The thing-doer's monobrow arched into an upside-down V. "Sorry," he muttered, mostly to himself. He quickly pulled his head in the window and shut it.

For a moment he thought about running after the widow's peaks and trying to talk them into giving his suit back. That would take a lot of effort, though, and the thing-doer didn't like to make a lot of effort in the morning. It took him an hour or so to fully wake up and become a fully motivated person with ambitions that he was willing to act on.

He retreated from the window, released the hammer of the .44. Returned to the kitchen to finish his breakfast.

As he got closer to finishing the doing of his morning things, the thing-doer become more and more anxious. What was he going to stare at all day in the mirror? A full head of hair, that's what. There was no point in staring at something like that. A full head of hair was nothing to focus his attention on because it was in no danger of becoming anything other than that which it already was, whereas a head of hair with two widening widow's peaks on it was in continuous danger of becoming something that it was not. But what did he care? He should have been happy that there was no longer a becoming-thing on his head. The likelihood of being bald as an ostrich egg in the not-too-distant future was now a steadfast unlikelihood. He should have smacked his lips in satisfaction and carried on with his life.

He didn't smack his lips. He had grown too accustomed to worrying about going bald. The sudden absence of that worry worried him more than he had ever worried before in his life.

When the last morning thing had been done, the thing-doer took his place in front of the mirror. There was no reason for him to do it, but he was a slave to Routine. If he broke the confines of Routine, well, that would just give him something else to worry about.

As he regarded the perfectly formatted, perfectly profuse strands of strong hair that inhabited either side of his forehead, the dark music of Pseudofolliculitis City drifted through the open window, reminding him of a past life...He winced, shuddered. It was a cruel world out there. Too cruel for most PCP, let alone things that are impersonating PCP.

He began to worry about the welfare of his widow's peaks. Were they OK? What were they doing out there in the world all by themselves? Was somebody taking advantage of them? Maybe they were taking advantage of somebody else. Or maybe they didn't want anything to do with anybody else. Were they at the movies? Were they feeding mutated pigeons pieces of old cereal? Were they sitting in the corner of an indiscreet Cuban café eating half-cooked pork, drinking Turkish coffee, staring at a stucco wall? Or were they sitting in the corner of a lizard lounge nursing a vodka luge while massaging the firm white thigh of a young lady? They could have been doing anything. They could have been window shopping for spectacles, befriending AIs, robbing a haberdashery, surfing the Schizoverse, taunting street mimes and organ grinders, joining a traveling band of dandies, pinching pieces of fruit in order to test their resilience, contemplating suicide, making a sandwich, filling out job applications, jetpacking across the troposphere, wandering through The Museum of Deep Meaning, riding an elevator to the roof of The Bigbamboom Tower, juggling bananas, arguing with a taxi driver, urinating in a dark alleyway...dying in a dark alleyway, their back a constellation of fresh stab wounds. Or dead in the trunk of a long blue Cadillac, their back a constellation of dried-up bullet holes...

For days on end, the thing-doer continued to wonder and worry about the widow's peaks. If he was not sleeping, eating, or doing his things, he was staring into the mirror at the reflection of his model-material hairline. Staring at it, and stressing out. And stressing out. And stressing out...

The notion that stress has the capacity to induce baldness is not applicable to all men. It requires a certain evil gene that vibrates in a certain evil way when it senses stress. This vibration prompts a man's scalp to either suck his hair into it or spit his hair out of it. Not all men have this gene. But the protagonist of this story does.

...One evening the thing-doer was in the middle of doing his evening things when he experienced a funny, tickling sensation on the top of his head. Expecting the best, he quickly spit his supper out of his mouth and hurried over to his mirror.

An ethereal sigh leaked out of the thing-doer's lips as he stroked the bald spot with a trembling pinky finger...

Duel

Two air guitarists were having a duel in Hootenanny Park. About ten feet of cobblestone divided them. Each man was biting his lip and banging his head as one of his hands fanatically thrummed the invisible strings of the lower portion of his invisible guitar while the fingers of his other hand tore up and down the invisible guitar's sizeable shaft in fasttime. Each man was also wearing a pair of thick-rimmed 3D glasses. They had been dueling all morning.

Surrounding the spectacle was a large body of PCP. Every now and then they would punch, elbow, and kick each other out of the way in order to gain a better viewpoint. A number of PCP had other PCP standing on their shoulders. A few PCP standing on other PCP's shoulders had other PCP standing on their shoulders.

Sitting at a long fold-out table in front of the spectacle was a committee of judges. The judges were the property of The Law, but given the symbolic nature of the duel, it was incumbent upon them to attend and play their systematic part. There were ten judges in all. Each of them was a Lyndon B. Johnson android, except for the judge-in-chief, Judge Wiffleflick, a genetically enhanced human who resembled a middle-aged Charleton Heston on steroids.

The air guitarists were fighting for the symbolic order of Interzone 342. If one of them prevailed, the Interzone would become a symbol of prosperity and goodwill, if the other prevailed, a symbol of degradation and assholery. Currently the Interzone was a symbol of mediocrity and indifference, a figurative state of being that, in the eyes of The Law, is not allowed to stand for more than half a year.

The actual state of being of the Interzone is of no consequence.

The air guitarists possessed the same mettle. One was no more talented or spirited than the other. They even had the same physiques, fashion senses, and mullet hairdos. The soon-to-be victor would depend upon the moods of the judges, namely Judge Wiffleflick, who, at the duel's conclusion, would have the final say-so. At the time he seemed to be in a good mood. There was a pleasant smile on his square leathery face, and his posture described a man who felt confident and refreshed. Periodically he would stand and flex his giant pectoral muscles in rapid succession as an affirmation of the air guitarists' hard work. Every once in awhile he would raise his hand in their air, make a hang loose sign with his fingers, and nod to the beat of the air music.

The duel continued for hours. The moat of PCP that surrounded it surged, growing taller and wider, as the table of judges oscillated between simulating wide-eyed attention and taking catnaps during which they snored like monsters. At one point a young, overexcited PCP started to play his own air guitar in an alleged attempt to prove that he was just as competent as the air guitarists in the limelight, both of whom held graduate degrees in air guitartistry, while he possessed a measly undergraduate degree in flâneury. This piece of public mimesis was not well-received by agents of The Law, who regarded mimesis as criminal behavior. A number of judges grabbed their mouths in surprise. Two policemen pointed at and shook their fingers at the impersonator. Judge Wiffleflick snarled, cursed, gnashed his teeth, leapt to his feet, shook his fist, removed a mace from within the folds of his robe and flung it end over end over end over end over...The mace struck the impersonator squarely in the face. His skull exploded and the PCP in his vicinity were splattered with black brains. His headless body remained standing for a moment, frozen in mid-strum, then collapsed to the ground and was immediately dragged away by the police. A few PCP threw up in disgust. Others urinated in fear. Others shrugged and wiped their eyes clean with the backs of their hands.

The air guitarists didn't miss a beat.

"Hiyaaaahhhh!!!" screamed Judge Wiffleflick, thrusting out his arm and flexing a massive bicep. The scream was both a warning to all potential air guitarist impersonators as well as an expression of delight that the duel was progressing in such an efficient manner.

Shortly thereafter, though, the air guitarists began to grow weary. Arthritic pain seeped into their furious hands and fingers. Vertigo began to set in, too. Their headbanging devolved into a woozy headflopping, and their firm, tall stances collapsed into round-shouldered slouches. Eventually they grew so tired they fell to the ground. Laying on their backs with their knees pointing at the sky, their fingers continued to flow up the invisible shafts of their air guitars, and their chins wiggled rhythmically. Granted, these gestures were executed in slow motion, but they were still executed, and as the last shred of verve and dynamism began to leak out of the air guitarists, the crowd began to hoot and holler and cheer and make orangutan noises, and the judges all stood up on their chairs and began to dance like excited chickens, flapping their arms and peck-pecking their heads and going "Bawk-bawk-bkaaawk," all except for the judge-in-chief of course, who opted to leap onto the table and dash up and down it like an Olympic sprinter, determined to reach his peak speed as mad squawks of delight surged out of his open mouth...

The air guitarists passed out at the same time. Their chins stopped wiggling, their arms fell to their sides, and they fell into a deep, dreaming sleep. One dreamt of squishing his toes into the cold wet sand of a cartoon beach. The other dreamt of waking up to find his partner casually masturbating next to him in bed.

As the dreams unfolded, the judges stopped rollicking. They huddled up to determine the victor and the ensuing new symbolic order that would be assigned to the city. Judge Wiffleflick presided over the huddle, repeatedly assuring the other judges that, no matter what their collective decision turned out to be, his decision would be the determining one whether it concurred with theirs or not. The crowd was still and silent, awaiting the final judgement...

Finally Judge Wiffleflick raised a tight fist over his head. He placed a bullhorn against his mouth, opened his fist, and announced the final judgement.

The chaos that followed was not an immoderate measure of chaos. There were a variety of reactions to the final judgement from a variety of PCP, ranging from blank-faced stares and eyebrow-raising to suicide by fire and machinegunfighting. Some do-badders were arrested by the police. Others were given dirty looks and told to behave themselves. Others were ignored. Whatever the case, by degrees the crowd calmed down and dispersed. And the police drove off in their paddywagons and on their unicycles. And the dead were dragged away by morticians and gravediggers. And the judges folded up their table and carried it back to the courthouse, Judge Wiffleflick leading the way with stately goosesteps. And a hobo walked onto the scene and began to dig through a garbage can overflowing with half-eaten hot dogs, caramel apples, containers of popcorn, bags of licorice...

And later, long after the sun had disappeared below the skyline of the city and the streets were empty, the air guitarists simultaneously stopped dreaming and awoke. They sat up. They stretched. They yawned. They stood up. They removed their 3D glasses. They blinked. They nodded at each other. They shook hands.

They walked away, their shadows changing shapes as they quietly passed beneath the streetlights.

Deli

The cashier is wearing a necklace that is supporting his late girlfriend's bleeding heart. He strangled her during his lunch break after she admitted she had been sleeping with the deli's sandwich-maker. After strangling her, he calmly used a butcher's knife to slice open her chest and remove her heart. He attached the heart to a string of leather, bowed his head, and slipped the necklace on, delighting in the symbolic nature of the act. Then he tossed his girlfriend's mangled corpse into a dumpster that was conveniently located 262 stories beneath her apartment window.

The sandwich-maker is standing in a shadow behind the cashier, making sandwiches. He doesn't know that his mistress has been murdered. That her bleeding heart is hanging from the cashier's neck, however, is making him a little suspicious. He'd know that bleeding heart anywhere. The way he is eyeing the back of the cashier's head is the way The Founder eyes the papanazzi the moment before their flashbulbs pop.

The walls have been painted deep, deep red by an artist named Clyde Von Wippleby. Coincidentally, Clyde happens to be sitting at a table in his dirty overalls eating a chicken salad sandwich. Bread crumbs are scattered like flakes of dandruff all over his burly Nietzschean mustache. He has no connection to the cashier or the sandwich-maker other than the fact that the sandwich-maker made his sandwich, the cashier charged him nine and a half doll hairs for it, and he is the grandfather of the cashier's late girlfriend. Unlike the sandwich-maker, the painter's attentiveness to the bleeding heart is ephemeral, confusing it as he does with a squalid, oversized amulet.

There is a picture on the wall. The picture depicts a murder. In one of the murderer's hands is a bleeding heart, in the other is a vegetarian sandwich.

There is Muzak in the air. The Muzak is fast-paced, edgy and metallic; at the same time, it possesses a certain soothing quality. It adequately reflects the present mental universe of the murderer in the picture as well as the murderer behind the cash register.

There are giant plasma TVs hanging from every ceiling corner. Each of the TVs is running different episodes of the same sitcom, and each episode sees the protagonist of the sitcom murdering his numerous girlfriends with numerous sharp objects. In between thrusts of the sharp objects, the protagonist often pauses, turns to the camera, and says something funny. All of the TVs have been muted so as not to clash with the Muzak, but close-captioned lines of script materialize at the bottom of the screens whenever the protagonist speaks, and whenever his girlfriends scream and curse, and whenever the laugh track sounds off.

At one table, a heart surgeon is trying not to think about the operation he screwed up that morning as he eats a bowl of psychedelic mushroom soup. He is still wearing his sky blue OR uniform, which is splattered in places with blood and viscera. When he purchased the soup from the cashier and saw the heart hanging from his neck, he thought the young man was taunting and making fun of him, but then he realized there was no way the cashier could have known that the heart surgeon had, just an hour ago, accidentally performed heart surgery on an errant lung he mistook for an errant heart. So he simply gave the cashier a dirty look.

At another table, an undercover detective is calling attention to his undercoverness by showcasing his prototypical gumshoe attire, which includes a banana yellow fedora, giant sunglasses, and a banana yellow trenchcoat with pointy shoulders. He is not investigating the murder of the cashier's late girlfriend, of course, since nobody officially knows it has occurred except for the cashier. Rather, he is investigating the murder in the painting on the wall. As he takes bites from his Italian submarine sandwich, he watches the painting out of the corner of his eyes, vigilantly, yet not so vigilantly that he is in danger of calling attention to himself with his eyes in addition to his attire. The moment he entered the deli he became so preoccupied with the painting that he failed to notice the bleeding heart hanging from the cashier's neck.

Sitting two tables away from the undercover detective are a salesman and his secretary. The secretary is a voluptuous Latinoid with tremendous breasts and long flaxen hair who the Caucazoid salesman with big hands and a JFK hairdo is clearly screwing on a regular basis. As they eat their respective egg salad and turkey club sandwiches, they are talking under their breaths to one another about how conspicuous the undercover detective is being about being an undercover detective, both with his not-so-covert vigilance as well as his gaudy Dick Tracy outfit. In addition, they are speculating about the authenticity of the cashier's peculiar necklace—neither of them believes it is real, but they're always open to new and improved possibilities—and they are smalltalking about the hogwild sex they are going to have on the salesman's desk when they return to the office. Little do they know that the salesman's wife will catch them in the act, kill them both, cut out their hearts and calmly eat them up with a knife and fork while taking sips from a glass of expensive cabernet sauvignon, delighting in the symbolic nature of the act.

There is only one more figure in the deli: a human-sized bleeding heart. The creature is sitting alone at a table. It is reading a newspaper with lobsterlike eyeballs. It is also smoking a cigarette and nibbling on a bleeding heart sandwich with an octopuslike beak. Nobody notices this figure, however, disconnected as they are from the goings-on of the real world.

Intermezzo

"A rhizome has no beginning or end; it is always in the middle, between things, interbeing, *intermezzo*."
                    —Deleuze & Guattari, *A Thousand Plateaus*

...explodes out a gaping manhole, does a graceful back flip in slow-mo and lands squarely, like an Olympic gymnast, on two strong feet. he quickly cracks his neck and rearranges his tie...and strikes a frail-looking bag lady underneath her chin with the blade of his hand, snapping her neck. a bloody machete flies helplessly out of the bag lady's dead claw as she flies end over end over end across the street as if awkwardly projected out of giant slingshot...a man in an Alfred Hitchcock fatsuit beheads three Russian mafioso thugs with a samurai sword in one swipe. the heads topple to the asphalt in slow-mo...speed up and splat. expressions of paralyzed confusion on their broken faces. their bodies continue to kung fu fight against the Alfred Hitchcock impersonator for fifteen more minutes until they realize their heads are lying on the ground like smashed pumpkins and they no longer belong to The Land Of The Living...black blood and cirrhotic innards spew out of neck holes...Dr. Dorian "Bling-Bling" Thunderlove dodges a deadly kick. slo-mo close-up on his livid B&W face...screaming ninjas in neonazi uniforms flip and fly across the expanse of the time-lapsing neon green sky...boy bands do breakdance moves and sing pop songs on street corners and rooftops...a brigade of wild-eyed late nineteenth century Men of Import wearing bowlers and handlebar mustaches and skintight Derridian suits goosestep down Giddyap Street...a brigade of blank-faced futique Men of Implode wearing stovepipe hats and isosceles triangle chin-beards and loose-fitting Boorskank Mexican tuxedos jetpack down Horrorshow Boulevard...flashbulb of infinite, inexplicable grotesqueries...naked jailbreakers smoke hubbly-bubbly in alleyways and smoke seeps out of their twitching lips, nostrils, ears in slo-mo...a roided up history professor tackles two kissass students, rips off their pencil-thin limbs, growls and flexes like the Hulk. he calmly removes a pair of chopsticks from his antiquated tweed jacket and dines on their eyeballs, dry-heaving with each tasteless swallow...pornstars descend from the heavens, exert a powerful deus ex machina, set everything in order. politicians immediately rise out of the gutters, return everything to shit and taxes...and gang-rape every last hardbodied evil-doer...a food fight breaks out in a sausage factory inducing uncontrollable penis envy in its female workers. giant razorsharp phalluses reflexively sprout from their crotches and attack anything that threatens their authority...MAN GORED BY GIANT PHALLUS THAT REFLEXIVELY SPROUTS OUT OF CO-WORKER'S CROTCH, reads a tabloid headline long before the atrocity takes place...a bug-eyed monster brandishes the old two-fingered peace sign as two air ragers leap out of their fan-gliders, fire up their jetpacks and square off with samurai swords. one of the air ragers is split in two from top to bottom—his halves slide apart with a slurp, black bile and bowels raining on the flyways...a tear rolls down the alien's scaly cheek. camera pops. the alien becomes a posterboy for The Blah Blah Blah Movement, gives motivational speeches in tall-steepled churches, sporting arenas, city squares, reality studios, taboo Interzones...[missing passage here: insert random act of ultraviolence]...purple blacklights stain the streets for miles and cast countless shadows of twitching stick figures...Dr. Thunderlove jabs, jabs, jabs, grins for the cameras, leaps into the air, does six fast-time backflips, weaves through the maelstrom of flesh, freeze-frames in midair. a random stranger scratches his head. the doctor bursts into realtime and bears down on the stranger's midsection with a karate chop from Hell. his insides pour out his mouth like a rainbow of sewage and the stranger slumps to the pavement, an empty shell, a hollow man, a BwO...five hundred million PCP yawn and scratch themselves...sentient skyscrapers spit infinite catwalks out of their window holes into the jungle of swinging construction beams out-side...inside the skyscraper that sits on the corner of Niminy and Piminy on the 498th floor of Interzone 13,833 across from restroom 111 in cubicle 230,856, an actuary with a concave chest, chronic hali-tosis and asymmetrical widow's peaks takes a delicate sip of steaming hot decaffeinated freeze-dried coffee from a thimble-sized styrofoam cup...wild packs of cheetahs and crocodiles gallop across the city preying on window shoppers...exploding fire hydrants...fistfuls of doll hairs...immeasurable breakdance and kung fu moves in slo-mo, in slower-mo...a thousand sleeping PBP dream the exact same dream at the exact same time...follicles spontaneously combusting...there's an empty stage, a spotlight, an audience cloaked in darkness. the audience nods and claps in fasttime by slamming strong index fingers into their wrinkled palms...wake up and freeze-frame...passing out to slo-mo and the audience detonates...gore...Thunderlove...irradiated skeletons erupting into the mirrored walls of the financial district...spectacle of scintillating crystals...spectacle of...

Bourgeois Man

Every good city has its superheros. Metropolis has Superman. Gotham has Batman. New York City has Spiderman, Daredevil. Atlantis has Aquaman. Hong Kong has Inframan...

Pseudofolliculitis City has Bourgeois Man.

Disgustingly handsome, ridiculously well-groomed, atrociously quick-witted, draped from head to toe in state-of-the-art Bling-Bling, able to amass commodities and fill out W-2 forms at lightning speed— Bourgeois Man is all this and more.

In this episode, we are introduced to our superhero as we are in every episode...Half-awake, he is hunched over a console, face-to-face with a computer screen, and dressed in his usual best: a striped clip-on tie and a white short-sleeved button-down. Surrounding him is the vastness of padded cells that constitutes Untitled Incorporated's cube farm...His name: Ulrich Underby. As always, he is viciously bored.

The computer screen contains an image.

It is his responsibility to stare at the image for no less than thirty minutes, then contact his superior, answer questions, and report his findings. Was the image offensive? Alluring? Blasé? How did it make him feel? Embarrassed? Afraid? Irate? Full of glee? Does the image remind him of anything or anybody? What? A rubber tree? Grover

Cleveland? How does he think other PCP might feel about the image? What kind of other PCP? PCP like him? What exactly is he like?...Following the Q&A, his superior will no doubt swear at him, even if he answers the questions to his liking, and then a new image will present itself on his screen to be interpreted.

Right now he is staring at a close-up picture of a plum. It is a good-looking plum; there doesn't seem to be an excess of discolorations or lesions on it. In spite of his boredom, he wonders if it is pink on the inside. And if so, how deep into the flesh of the fruit does the pink go?...

It hasn't always been this way. Once Ulrich had a real job. A job that not only allowed him to stare at and interpret things, but to actually make things. He was in the numbers business. An accountant, they called him. All day long he got to add and subtract and multiply and divide numbers and make them into new numbers. It was fulfilling work, and his paycheck, while nothing to smile at, was nothing to scoff at either. He had a wife, too. Betty Lomax-Underby. She loved him almost as much as she loved his paycheck.

The good life came to an abrupt halt one night when Ulrich was working late.

His employer at the time, Boondoggler Industries, specialized in the development of corporate logos. It had offended a certain bioterrorist group with a certain piece of anti-bioterrorist advertising, prompting them to nuke their corporate headquarters. Ulrich luckily finished his work long before the building went up in flames, but he unluckily slipped and fell into a NWP (Nuclear Waste Puddle) on his way home. NWPs are randomly positioned by The Law on the streets, sidewalks, alleyways, and rooftops of Pseudofolliculitis City, a technique The Founder of the city has been quoted as somewhat facetiously saying "is meant to keep follicles on their toes." This particular NWP balanced out a chemical unbalance that had already existed in his system and permitted him to excel in certain contexts as a functional capitalist. It produced a metabolic change in his body, a change that occurred whenever anti-capitalist villainy reared its ugly head. Curiously, it also furnished him with superhuman social skills and an adept knowledge of Jeet Kune Do, Bruce Lee style. Not a bad turnout for a slip and a fall. But shortly after the bioterrorist attack on Boondoggler Industries headquarters, the company was forced to make a few cutbacks here and there, and Ulrich's position was one of them. Betty was less than pleased. She left him that night, became a stripper, befriended a homely and elderly but wealthy entrepreneur whose job was in no danger of being yanked out from beneath his feet, remarried, and lived indifferently ever after.

That had been over five years ago. Ulrich still thinks about Betty on occasion. The monotony of his job provides him with plenty of time to daydream and rue the past. At first, it was difficult to focus on his work; his superior threatened to fire him routinely. Then he started getting drunk every night and hung over the next day...The headaches and nausea inhibited the process of daydreaming, and his superior resigned to mere name-calling and making cracks about his lack of masculinity. It was for the best. Bourgeois Man, after all, has enemies. Regardless of how much he resents Betty for being a superficial bitch, he does not want to be responsible for any injury, mortal or otherwise, that might befall her.

Back to our current episode. The final image Ulrich must interpret for the day is a head shot of talk show host Rackman Hackman. The man is smiling like a horse, and his leaning-tower-of-Pisa pompadour hairdo is threatening to tip over onto his face. Like the plum, he wonders if the hairdo is pink on the inside...

He phones his superior, Benjamin Hooha, and they run through their routine.

"I think this and I feel that," says Ulrich.

"I see," replies his superior. "But what do you feel about this and what do you think about that?"

"Blah blah blah."

"Right. Well then. That'll be all, Mr. Underby. Piss off for the day."

"Thank you, sir."

"I said piss off, shithead! I didn't ask for a thank you and I don't want one!"

"My apologies, sir."

"Shove your apologies up your ass, loser!"

"Right away, Mr. Hooha."

His superior screams indistinctly before hanging up. Ulrich calmly follows his lead.

He shuts down his workstation and begins the long process of finding his way out of the maze of Untitled Inc.'s cube farm, the structure of which is mechanically altered day by day in an effort to disallow employees from growing acclimatized to their environment. As the billboard that hangs over the front door of the company says: ACCLIMATIZATION IS THE SPINE OF SLOTH.

It takes him thirty minutes to get to the exit portal. He waits in line as his coworkers rummage through their lockers, screw in earplugs, strap on jetpacks...When he finally gets to his locker, it won't open. He tells it to scan his retina again. It still won't open. "You are not Ulrich Underby," the locker says to him. "You are an imposter."

Ulrich flexes his jaw. "Open up."

"And you are ugly."

His expression sours. "That's the best you can do? Call me ugly?"

A series of motorized spitting sounds as the locker ruminates. Finally it says: "Fucker."

Ulrich pounds on it. "Open up!"

"Ouch. That hurts me, my friend."

Ulrich glances over his shoulder and smiles uncomfortably at the line of employees that is waiting to get by him. Each of his co-workers is staring him down with their own uniquely annoyed and disgusted face. "Sorry," he squeaks.

He turns back to the locker and commands its obedience. It continues to dillydally with him for a bit longer before complying. Ulrich removes his jetpack and a box of Third World Hellfires from it. He tries to slam the door, but the locker tenses up its joints and won't let him. "Ah ah ah," it says.

"Smartass AIs," he grumbles.

He hammers the BRB (Big Red Button) with his palm and the exit door irises open. He slips on his jetpack, yanks its ignition cord. He opens the box of Hellfires, taps out a cigarette, lights it.

He takes a deep drag and leaps into the city...

Untitled Inc. is located on the 601st floor of the Van Locken Building between 16,244th and Rumplestiltskin Streets on the east side of Ladeeda Way. Ulrich lives in a $1/4$-bedroom apartment on the 601st floor of the Gaston del Merde Building, coincidentally, which is only about 1,000 or so blocks down Rumplestiltskin. The coffee shop he likes to drop by on his way home, Brown Town, a new chain featuring discounted MaHuang espressos, can be found 422 blocks down

Rumplestiltskin and three blocks up Ricky Ticky Tavy Avey on the 553rd floor of Ivory Tower #6. Traffic permitting (including the lines at the coffee shop), it usually takes him about an hour and fifty-five minutes to get to his front door.

Hovering in Untitled airspace, Ulrich slips on a pair of small, circular mirrorshades as he smokes his Hellfire and gauges which thoroughfare will be the most accessible. The apocalyptic roar of engines is everywhere and seems to resonate in his body from the inside-out rather than the other way around. His earplugs don't do much to ward it off. They're outmoded Clamorhammers, model Z341.56. He's owned them for over six months now. The Z341.56s only last for two, three months at most before going bad, not to mention that Pseudofolliculitis City's noise level increases daily as more traffic continues to flood the skyways, rendering even the best models inadequate after just a short while. He's been saving up for state-of-the-art Clamorhammers, Hammertime Edition. Upgrades aren't cheap, but he needs to get on the ball: right now he'd probably do just as well to stick a couple of spitballs in his ears. As he dangles there in the veins of the windy cityscape, a headache overcomes him almost immediately.

Beneath and above him the city is an interminable labyrinth of glinting catwalks, slidewalks and airways buzzing with jetpackers, taxis, gondolas, airbuses, airboats, speedracers, fangliders, hot air balloons, zeppelins, antique fighter planes, turbogoblins, cloud cars, punk rockets, willowinds, hang tanks, gigantic mechanical pterodactyls (the attack vehicles of The Law), SUVs (Skydiving Ultralight Velocipedes)...Interzone 2,609 is a jungle. But then again so are most of Pseudofolliculitis City's Interzones, except for a select few that are preserved as national parks and dinosaur clone sanctuaries, and others that are quarantined because black holes have grown there. A recent poll says that approximately 6,054.2 jetpackers per day are killed during rush hour in public Interzones. No big loss— more than twice that number are cloned every day, and as The Law sees it, it's simply one means of population control (another includes executing follicles who forget to put their makeup on in the morning). It's a risky business, going to and from work. But vehicles are expensive, the lowliest junkers costing as much as a year's rent in a modest $1/4$-bedroom apartment, and jetpacks are cheap, a standard model costing as little as ninety-nine and a half doll hairs.

On his way to Brown Town Ulrich is nearly killed on three occasions, two below his average. On the first, a taxi collides head-on with a turbogoblin not ten feet in front of him, and he is just able to dodge the resulting implosion (at high enough speeds, turbogoblins assimilate objects on impact). On the second, a jetpacking grandmother with a blue beehive hairdo flying at a snail's pace refuses to let him pass her. When he finally does pass her, she gets mad and chases him for over twenty blocks, hurling a seemingly endless supply of butcher's knives at his back. On the third, a policeman decides to terminate him for no apparent reason. Sitting behind the neon red eyes of a pterodactyl with a demonic yellow grin on his Churchillian face, the cop swoops down on him, snatches him up with a rusty metal claw, squeezes and shakes him, shouts obscenities at him out of a loudspeaker, tells him he is guilty of existing, and lifts him to the gallows that is the pterodactyl's great metallic beak. Luckily, just before his head is bitten off, a fanglider accidentally crashes into the pterodactyl's head. Ulrich scurries out of the machine's claw like a minnow in water as its head explodes and its body falls into the deep, electric strata of traffic below...

By the time he reaches the coffee shop, he's altogether pooped. He touches down on Brown Town's landing circle like a maladroit, uncoordinated teenager, clumsily bumping into a group of zoots and tripping over his own feet. He topples onto his face. The zoots swear at him in their native language, dust off and rearrange their colorful garments, swear at him in pseudospeak, secure their jetpacks, guzzle what remains of the coffee they had been drinking, swear at him in Thoidy-Thoid-n-Thoid (a language that only exists at the crossroads of 33rd and 3rd), and leap into traffic. Ulrich swears at himself as he gets to his feet and shakes the stars out of his eyes. Once he can see straight again, he combs his hair into place with his fingers, weaves through a crowd of dandies and flâneurs with their eyelids and lips nailed into their faces, and disappears into a revolving mirrordoor...

Inside of Brown Town is a large, triangular cafeteria strewn with futique, pencil-thin furniture. The walls are decorated in state-of-the-art PPCOG (Psychedelic Pornographic Clockwork Orange Graffiti), and each wall has its own purpose. One of them is a pissoir and contains a long line of ornate troughs. Another contains outlets and cranial shunts for customers to jack into the Schizoverse. Embedded in the third wall is a kitchen where an orderly queue of barristabots are ringing up orders and serving customers beverages. The barristabots are shiny, metallic stick figures with wiry appendages constructed out of the same materials as the furniture. Screwed onto their shoulders, however, are clones of extinct bird heads including the passenger pigeon, the kago, the dodo, the kakapo, the monkey-eating eagle, the peregrine falcon, the takahé, the piping plover, and the vegan buzzard. The proprietors of Brown Town employ the heads for what they perceive to be a shrewd marketing tool: not only do they present their customers with the opportunity to enjoy stimulating refreshments at unreasonable prices, they also present them with pieces of the past.

The moment he enters the coffee shop, Ulrich senses a disturbance. It isn't because he is particularly shrewd. Any idiot can tell that something is awry. Usually the place is a madhouse, full of customers gibbering, shouting, laughing, slurping, belching, slapping their knees, slapping each other on the backs, clearing their throats, and holding conversations at the top of their lungs. This is the antithesis of that scene. Some customers are sitting down drinking their coffee, others are standing up. Others are urinating in the pissoir. But very few of them are speaking to one another. And if they are speaking, it is in a quiet, controlled, yet somehow terrorized whisper; and the composite tenor of everybody's whisperings is barely making a dent in the sound of the low-level sensurround Muzak that saturates the place. Everybody is particularly stiff-looking, too, exhibiting wide eyes and pricked up ears, as if they have been poked in the back by a sharp stick.

Frowning, Ulrich ambles toward the barristabots, fighting off vertigo. It seems the floor might give way beneath him at any moment. He has a bad feeling in his gut—the kind of feeling he gets when something anti-capitalist is looming in the air.

His feeling is soon confirmed, and he stops in his tracks. Out of the corners of his eyes he sees him. On the other side of the room, in front of a tall stained glass window, underneath a powerful blacklight...it is his arch-nemesis. It is every PCP's arch-nemesis.

The Tax Collector.

His nose is hooked like a beak, his back is as crooked as The Law, his eyes are yellower than Hellfire executive Horace P. Rottenbum's nicotine-stained smile, his corroded-looking skin is an amphibious green color...If the creature were naked and you sized him up with a glance, you would no doubt mistake him for a giant, demonic bullfrog standing on its hind legs. But he isn't naked. He's wearing a dark broad-shouldered suit, thick black spectacles, and a fedora slightly tilted to one side. He's also wearing a low-grade cologne that, coupled with his special brand of BO, produces a scent reminiscent of rotten sausage. He looks like a cross between the Wicked Witch of the West and Clark Kent, and anybody he speaks to, despite their fear of upsetting him, can't stop themselves from reacting to his stench by making sour faces, pinching their noses, twitching their brows and lips...

He is speaking to a man now. The man is sitting at a table by himself, and The Tax Collector is leaning over him, whispering something in his ear. Whispering something foul, of course, something related to a debt he very likely doesn't owe but will be required to pay at risk of the penalty of public humiliation and subsequent defragmentation...Ulrich has seen it happen many times before, and while he has fought valiantly against The Tax Collector, he has never been able to rid the city of his socioeconomic curse. He is a primordial minion of The Law, after all, not to mention that he is, like many of The Law's minions, an undead zombie, genetically created by the government's army of mad scientists to antagonize the general public and disturb the waters of Pseudofolliculitis City's commoditocracy. Still, whenever their paths cross, Ulrich is helpless to the doppelgänger that falling into the NWP has awakened in him. Whenever he crosses paths with any form of anti-capitalism, he can't stop his mind and body from changing...changing from the meek, soft-spoken, listless husk of an everyman into a dynamic presence capable of reestablishing the capitalist flow of desire, if only momentarily.

Watching The Tax Collector, he can feel himself changing now. It always happens very quickly. He can feel his banal outfit convulsing, stiffening up, evolving from a cheap dimestore garment into an extravagant three-piece Frickleminn business suit. Likewise does his bargain-priced, short-sleeved shirt evolve into a dapper, long-sleeved Speildenrogue oxford, and his clip-on tie loses its corny stripes, becomes a solid blood-colored streak that nestles into his vest as its fabric wraps itself around the inner collar of his shirt like a pet snake. His worn out mocksiders are overtaken by spit-shined wingtips. The gold chain of a pocketwatch, elegant cuff links, and modish rings sprout into existence. Then, his body...His hairy, white potbelly tightens up into a smooth, tan sixpack. With a crack his spine straightens into a strong two-by-four. Sound of a cool breeze as his tousled mop of a hairdo slicks back against his scalp, and then a bowler crawls out of his suit collar like an inch-worm and positions itself atop the new locks. His pale, flaking skin turns bronze and silky smooth, as if he has been applying top notch anti-aging skin products to it every day since his mother let him loose...Finally a thick, handsomely groomed handlebar mustache pops onto his overlip, and he grins the bright white grin of a movie star. Not a bird, not a plane.

Bourgeois Man.

When the transformation is over, a young boy immediately recognizes him. He pokes his father in the ribs, points at the superhero, and shouts, "Hey! It's Bourgeois Man!"

The Muzak abruptly squeaks off as the occupants of Brown Town, human and robot alike, freeze and fix their gazes on him. Even the man The Tax Collector is beleaguering glances in his direction, although guardedly.

The Tax Collector snarls, dropping the cup of MaHuang espresso with poi sprinkles he has been holding. The cup falls to the floor and explodes in slow motion...

"*You*," he growls.

A path clears like the parting of the Red Sea in fasttime between the two rivals. The Tax Collector grimaces, bears his skanky teeth, shakes his ham-fists, stomps his black shoes in a fit of childish rage. Bourgeois Man continues to beam with confidence. Arching his back, folding his arms across his chest, tilting back his head, broadening his brilliant smile, emitting an overpowering and unmitigated aura of Bling-Bling, he says, "Let that man drink his coffee, fiend."

The Tax Collector screams. The scream is a raging earthquake. Customers cover their ears and accidentally bite off their tongues as glassware shatters, windows crack, the room shakes...The scream abruptly ends. Severed tongues flip-flop on the floor like goldfish out of water. The Tax Collector clears his throat. Grins like a skull.

"That's no way to greet an old friend," he seethes.

Bourgeois Man ignores him. "I said leave that man alone."

"You know I can't do that," retorts The Tax Collector. "This man has obligations. This man must pay the piper, hee hee. All men must pay the piper, hee hee."

In an immaculate, flawlessly articulated tone of voice decorated in a mildly discernable (but by no means egregious) Old English accent, Bourgeois Man replies, "Hee hee yourself."

The Tax Collector smirks.

Bourgeois Man nods.

The Tax Collector grabs the man by the back of the head and smashes his face into the table in front of him. Like the cup of coffee, the face explodes in slow motion...

Whereas he maintains his powerful stance, Bourgeois Man's smile disappears. "That wasn't a very polite thing to do."

"Up yours, *Bee* Man," snorts The Tax Collector, shaking the gore off of his hand.

Bourgeois Man slowly begins walking forward. Everybody watches him expectantly. A few customers slip out the front door. Others cram jacks into their heads and retreat into the Schizoverse. Some dive into the kitchen and the pissoir, quivering in fear.

Bourgeois Man says, "Listen to me. I don't want any trouble. Nobody wants any trouble. Let's simply talk this matter out, shall we? Let's talk it out like gentlemen. Underneath your brazenly unctuous, fetid and altogether nauseating exterior, I know there is a gentleman waiting to be unleashed. Stout fellow! I know you want to do the right thing. I'll even treat you to a coffee, if you please. I might even be persuaded to purchase you a sandwich. If I'm not mistaken, dog salad croissants are on special today. Nothing like the taste of man's best friend to brighten your mood, eh? How does that sound then?"

He knows what the answer is, of course. Everybody knows. And The Tax Collector knows that Bourgeois Man and everybody knows. He knows that they know he knows, too. But as a matter of course, it is incumbent upon Bourgeois Man, as both a superhero and a gentleman himself, to attempt to neutralize all criminal activity first by means of the Word, then by the Fist. There is absolutely *no* question that the power of language will *not* lead to a resolution of the conflict. In Pseudofolliculitis City, conflicts are almost always resolved by acts of physical violence. To not resolve a conflict in such a way is illegal. If a PCP is suspected by The Law of not resolving more than five conflicts in a row by acts of physical violence, the punishment is a partial lobotomy that erases most of the lexicon and produces a powerful stutter, ensuring that the PCP will never be able to sweet talk its way out of anything again...

In response to Bourgeois Man's offer, The Tax Collector belches. The stench of the belch strikes a customer in the face, instantly suffocating him. The Tax Collector takes a garish bow...and then nimbly leaps at another customer, tears off his nose, throws it on the floor, and stomps on it with his heel. The customer's nose is torn off so swiftly he doesn't realize it at first, and he wonders why there are filaments of blood squirting out of his face. Then it hits him. Before he can react, The Tax Collector deals him a fasttime roundhouse kick that takes his head off. His body stands there for a second, confused, and then collapses. His head rolls across the floor and strikes Bourgeois Man on the toe of one of his wingtips, marking it with blood and a piece of flesh.

Bourgeois Man stops walking forward as if freeze-framed. He glances back and forth between The Tax Collector and his defamed shoe with round, bemused eyes. Enjoying his distress, The Tax Collector claps his hands together, bleating, "Hee hee! Hee hee! Hee hee!"

"How dare you, sir," says Bourgeois Man calmly, without emotion, as if he doesn't really care. But he does care. Attacking his fashion statement is not a wise thing for any man, dead or alive, to do. Attack his family, attack his bank account, attack his ideology. But do not attack his finery. Excusing himself, he removes a Bladderfield handkerchief from his pocket, lifts up his foot, grips it by the heel, and wipes the gore from his toe, looking like a well-dressed flamingo. Unlike the cumbersome Ulrich, Bourgeois Man is very flexible. During the cleaning process, a few more customers sneak out the door, jack into the Schizoverse, crawl into the pissoir...When he's finished, Bourgeois Man breathes on and buffs the shoe until its sheen returns. He releases his foot, tosses aside the handkerchief, pushes back his shoulders, cracks his neck, and grins. "Not very polite, no, not very polite," he intones, and arranges himself into a formless Jeet Kune Do stance, his dancing feet flowing in slow motion as his fists of fury ready themselves, slicing through the air like long, angry insects.

The Tax Collector points at him dramatically. He throws back his head, flashes his eyes. Slowly he turns his finger over and uses it to beckon his enemy...

The fight lasts 105 minutes in slow motion, thirty minutes in real-time, and forty-four seconds in fasttime. A customer listening to it from outside is later quoted by *People!!!* magazine as saying it was mainly characterized by the sound of "crashing furniture," "exploding heads," "Bruce Lee noises," and "Hee hees!" Customers who actually witness and survive the fight confirm the characterization, although one of them adds: "There were also short pauses when Bee Man and Taxy would get tired, take coffee breaks, and discuss the weather..."

In the end, Bourgeois Man ends up wounding The Tax Collector. A blow to his neck shatters his Adam's apple, and the creature slumps into a pile of bones, gagging and spitting and vomiting up pieces of cartilage...Bourgeois Man grabs him by the scruff and picks him up. Smiling in triumph, he says, "Why do you do what you do, Taxy?"

The Tax Collector shrugs his shoulders. "It's my job," he breathes...and kicks Bourgeois Man in the balls.

Bourgeois Man doubles-over. "Unsportsmanlike!" he squeals.

The Tax Collector's neck cracks and squeaks as his head spins around his shoulders like a rotisserie. "That's the name of my game.

We'll meet again, Bee Man. I promise you!" Confiscating Bourgeois Man's numerous articles of Bling-Bling in the name of The Law, The Tax Collector tears off his suit coat, exposing a small single-engine jetpack, and leaps through a stained glass window. His giggles doppler away for a moment before disappearing into the caterwaul of traffic...

Bourgeois Man passes out. By the time he regains consciousness, he has metamorphosed back into Ulrich. No more gentlemanly accouterments, no more athletic physique. No more handlebar mustache.

His vision is white. A sheet is laying on his face. He blows it off...Human and robot janitors are scurrying all over Brown Town, sweeping and squeegeeing up its carnage. Barristabots are self-cleaning their joints with long, synthetic tongues that skillfully dart out of their bird-heads. Policemen are idly drinking coffee, talking to witnesses, and goosing one another. Nobody has recognized Ulrich— not as Bourgeois Man, not as a living human being...He quickly but unassumingly gets up, locates his jetpack, and slips out the jagged hole in the window that The Tax Collector left behind.

As he hovers in the air and surveys the vast infrastructure of the city, his theme song begins to play. He puts on his mirrorshades. He lights a Hellfire, takes a deep drag. The song drowns out the sound of traffic, and he waits for it to finish before flicking away his cigarette, inserting his Clamorhammers, swandiving into a flyway, and allowing the credits, advertisements, deleted scenes, alternate endings, and language selections to roll...

Cereal Killers

A man decided to become a serial killer. His target: all of the cereal killers in the city whose many victims included various new and improved brands names...

"It's the same old shit!" was the cereal killers' logic.

"I'm bored," was the man's logic.

"This is problematic," was what a dandy said when he read about the serial killings in the newspaper. Because after all of the cereal killers were dead, there was no longer any means of population control. New and improved brands of cereal multiplied like tribbles. Soon the city was infested and there was nothing anybody could do about it except sit down in their kitchens and quietly eat their new and improved breakfasts.

And so the man decided to become a cereal killer. "The city needs me," was his logic.

"Who needs a job when you've got the Bling-Bling?" was the dandy's logic.

"Ouch!" was what the boxes of cereal exclaimed when the man's bullets pierced their delicate skin...

fascists

A handful of fascists fell out of the sky and landed in a numberless Interzone. They were wearing skintight five-star-general uniforms, and their thick black manes were slicked back across their scalps with a brand of extinct lard that they had purchased from a discount store in their native imaginary universe.

"It's raining fascists!" exclaimed a PCP as bodies hit the sidewalk all around him. He removed an umbrella from his briefcase, opened it over his head, and hurriedly skulked away.

The fall knocked the fascists unconscious. They lay there on the sidewalk in contorted, uncomfortable-looking positions for half an hour. Fascinated by the spectacle of their scattered bodies, street-walkers passed by them slowly, vigilantly, as if they were a car accident.

When they woke up, the fascists removed miniature pink feather dusters from their pockets and cleaned the grit off of each other. They re-slicked back their hair with fresh doses of lard.

"Right," said the fascist in charge, glancing purposefully at his comrades. "To work, then."

The directive prompted the other fascists to begin twitching uncontrollably, their obsession with order kicking in like a bad acid trip. The twitching quickly subsided, however, and each of them grabbed a random streetwalker by the shoulder, commanding him to get down on his hands and knees. "You are my soap box!" they shouted. Having nothing better to do than walk the streets, the streetwalkers acquiesced without an unreasonable amount of bitching.

The fascists stepped onto the streetwalkers' backs. They stood there for a moment in silence, collecting their thoughts and observing the ebb and flow of mortal commerce. Then they opened their mouths and unleashed their dogma...

Their bodies gesticulated. Their fists hammered the air. Their mustaches convulsed as they spat things like "Chaos is dead!" and "This is the end of image-addiction!" and "I am the power!" and "Death to the implosion of the social!"

After awhile the streetwalkers cum soap boxes began to get sore backs. Most of them were reticent to complain about it at first, but eventually they were all snivelling and whining out loud.

Their bodies quivered. Their fingertips dug into the pavement. Their upper lips broke out in mustaches of sweat as they spat things like "Pain is my enemy!" and "This is not very healthy for my spine!" and "I am going to cry!" and "Death to the bastard on top of me!"

A crowd gathered around this display of verbal pyrotechnics. Initially the crowd just stared on in dumb wonderment. Then PCP started flipping quarters at the fascists. A few of them tossed sandwiches in their direction.

"We don't want your coins or your lunches!" the fascist in charge screamed. "We want you to flush your ideology down the toilet!"

But nobody heard him clearly enough to mind him. The fascists and the soap boxes were simultaneously hollering at the top of their lungs, and their words collapsed and crashed into one another like stormy ocean waves. Some PCP had to plug their ears, the clamor was so loud and obnoxious, albeit they continued to shower the spectacle with booty...

The Autopsy

A mesomorph was pretending to be a corpse. He lay on an elevated slab of concrete, breathing through his pores...

A trap door in the crystal floor fell open and Dr. Thunderlove levitated into the room. "Good afternoon, gentlemen," he announced. The gentlemen nodded politely. They were wearing antiquated frock coats and trousers and constituted the walls and ceiling of the room— their long, elastic appendages had been threaded together like wicker into a great igloo shape. All of the gentlemen were skilled contortionists. Grafted onto their faces were celluloid Thunderlove masks. The only difference between the masks and the doctor's face was that they were equipped with caricatured noses and chins.

The butcher's knife Dr. Thunderlove held in his hand was the size of a snow shovel. He sharpened it with a stick of steel as he strode over to the mesomorph...

Next to the slab of concrete was a nightstand containing a sleek, dimly lit Victorian lamp. It was the only light source in the room. Dr. Thunderlove tossed the stick of steel aside and carefully lay the butcher's knife down on the nightstand. He spit in his palms, rubbed his hands together, cracked his knuckles one at a time. During the process he told a few dirty jokes to his audience.

In response to each joke, the gentlemen mechanically opened their mouths and monotoned, "Ha-ha-ha-ha-ha-ha-ha-ha-ha-ha-ha-ha-ha-ha-ha-ha." They closed their mouths.

Despite his friendly smile and soft brown eyes, Dr. Thunderlove's sharp, birdlike face looked vaguely demonic in the faint light of the lamp. He wore a skintight pale green OR uniform, a long black cape with a stiff collar that rose above his ears, a tall top hat, and a fake handlebar mustache. His physique belonged to a chemically enhanced bodybuilder. Every now and then an overgrown pectoral muscle would flex of its own volition.

The mesomorph had rolled his open eyes back into his head. He was entirely naked except for the ring he wore on his pinky toe. Hanging from the ring by a string was a plagiarized coroner's note that read:

To Whom It May Concern:

The body attached to this note is dead (that is to say, not alive). Handle with care. In light of the aforementioned condition of the body, however, an inordinate amount of care is unnecessary. No care at all is necessary, if you prefer.

Sincerely,
None Of Your Business

Unlike the doctor, the mesomorph's physique was nothing to double-take, although it was somewhat muscular, or at least sinewy, particularly in the abdominal region: his six-pack was as acute as an

148

armadillo's back. His body had been waxed and spitshined. His terminal genital lounged across one of his thighs as if taking a nap.

The terminal nature of the genital was the first thing Dr. Thunderlove spotted. "I see," he said to himself. He removed a small pad of paper and a mechanical pencil from his cape and scribbled down a note-to-self. He continued to take notes-to-self as he inspected the rest of the mesomorph's body, extremity by extremity. The last extremity he inspected was his head. When he was finished, he drew this:

He returned the pad of paper and the pencil to his cape. "Right. Shall we begin?"

"Let's begin," droned his audience.

As Dr. Thunderlove reached for the butcher's knife, the mesomorph accidentally blinked and his eyes rolled into place. He quickly threw them back up into his head, but not before Dr. Thunderlove had caught him red-handed. The doctor frowned, rearranged his lips, leaned over, and whispered in his ear.

"Liar," he whispered.

No response. The eyes remained white, the body still. It was getting more and more difficult not to breathe. He had been breathing through his pores instead of his mouth for awhile now. The microscopic pores couldn't be seen taking breaths, of course, and so their stealth was safe from immediate exposure. But fatigue had set in. The pores weren't used to breathing. Their muscles were beginning to cramp up...

Dr. Thunderlove shook his head. He knew the mesomorph was pretending to be a corpse. He told him so. "You're not fooling me. You're not fooling anybody. Play dead all you want. *Everybody knows you're alive.*"

The mesomorph momentarily allowed his eyes to return to their normal position. He stared at the doctor. He shot alert glances at the faces of the gentlemen who constituted the room to see if they were wise to his scheme. They were. A few of the gentlemen shook their heads at him disapprovingly. Others called him a bastard and an asshole.

He stared at the doctor again. "I'm sorry?" he whispered.

Dr. Thunderlove smiled a crooked smile. "I don't think so."

"Can't you just pretend that I'm not pretending to be a corpse? I promise I won't move. I won't make a peep. You have my word."

"It doesn't matter, your word. The autopsy will proceed as scheduled."

"Thank you."

The doctor's lips peeled back over his teeth. "*Silence,*" he said, raising his voice. "You are embarrassing yourself. You are at risk of embarrassing me, I tell you."

The mesomorph apologized again, sincerely this time. Dr. Thunderlove begrudgingly accepted the apology. The mesomorph asked if he could keep his eyes closed rather than roll them back into his head. Dr. Thunderlove said, "Fine." The mesomorph asked if it would be all right if he could breath through his nostrils or mouth. Dr. Thunderlove said, "No." Even though everybody knew he was a phony, he couldn't appear to be noticeably breathing. The mesomorph asked why. Dr. Thunderlove said, "Because The Law is The Law." The mesomorph sighed, closed his eyes, and returned to breathing through his worn-out pores.

The doctor tilted up his head. "Very well, gentlemen. And now we shall begin the autopsy proper."

As they did not have use of their tied-together limbs, the gentlemen clicked their tongues in applause. Dr. Thunderlove pushed his lips out into a rosebud shape and gave his audience a single, deep nod. He shrugged off his cape, nodded again, hunched over, and flexed the muscles in his upper body. The exoskeleton of purple veins that covered his stainless steel flesh flared up like a school of excited eels as his shirt ripped, shredded, exploded into confetti.

Virtually all of the gentlemen made fascinated frog faces. "My my my," said one of them.

Dr. Thunderlove smiled, bowed. In one smooth motion he retrieved the butcher's knife, swung it over his head, and expertly slammed the blade into the mesomorph's chest.

"Ouch," said the mesomorph matter of factly.

The doctor ignored him. He used the knife like a handsaw to dutifully cut from the clavicle all the way down to the pubis. "Ouch," said the mesomorph with each sawing motion. "Ouch. Ouch. Ouch. Ouch. Ouch."

"Knock it off," fumed the doctor, removing the blade.

"I can't help it," replied the mesomorph. "It hurts me."

The doctor's fake mustache twitched. He cracked his neck in frustration. His top hat tipped to one side of his head. He didn't straighten it out.

He slammed the knife into the mesomorph's chest and sawed him open horizontally...The mesomorph cried out in pain as his rib cage collapsed.

Dr. Thunderlove placed the knife back on the nightstand. He

opened a drawer, removed a pair of oversized sunglasses, slid them on. Blood was bubbling and seeping out of the mesomorph's wounds, but it wasn't squirting. It didn't start squirting until the doctor grabbed the mesomorph by the flaps of the vertical slit in his chest and tore him open like a Christmas present.

"Pardon the gratuitous violence," the doctor smirked as a dark tan was sprayed onto his face, pectorals, arms and abdomen. The gentlemen smirked back. The doctor made no effort to shield himself, allowing the gore to wash over him until it subsided. Black blood oozed and trickled down the grooves of his musculature, dripped off the tips of his nose, chin, nipples, elbows...

The mesomorph croaked, "I don't feel very well."

Dr. Thunderlove removed the blood-splattered sunglasses, fussily cleaned them with a handkerchief, and returned them to the drawer. He opened another drawer and removed a large hammer and two rusty railroad tie nails. He butterflied the mesomorph, stretching the flaps of his torso onto the concrete slab and pounding a nail into each of them. It was a long, tedious process. The concrete wasn't impenetrable, but it wasn't accommodating either.

The mesomorph demonstrated a surprising lack of whining and squirming during the process. For a moment, the doctor suspected he might have actually died. Then the mesomorph whispered, "The breeze...the breeze is tickling my organs. Make it stop, sir. Please."

"There's no breeze in this place. This room is tightly sealed. The only breeze your organs could possibly be experiencing is the breath coming out of my mouth when I exhale, which is impossible as my mouth is not aimed at your organs. You're feeling things that aren't there. At any rate, clam up. Stop playing alive already."

"But I am alive. I'm playing dead. You told me to play dead."

"What you play is your own affair despite what you claim I do or do not tell you."

The mesomorph made an attempt to respond. Dr. Thunderlove threw his arms in the air and exclaimed, "Silence, fiend! Silence, whore! Silence, you sonuvabitch!"

The mesomorph reluctantly obeyed. His terminal genital, on the other hand, rose to attention like a flag.

Infuriated to the nth degree, now the doctor exclaimed, "Down, fiend! Down, whore! Down, you sonuvabitch!"

By degrees the genital receded, slumping back into its lazy ways...

A long, uncomfortable silence followed. A few of the gentlemen grew bored and began to stick their tongues out at one another, without provocation at first, then as a method of retaliation for having had tongues stuck out at them. It wasn't long before all of the gentlemen were sticking their tongues out like angry snakes, adjusting the position of their heads with insectlike jerks to make certain that each antagonist got what was coming to him.

Eventually Dr. Thunderlove tuned in to the gentlemen's childish antics. "Knock off that hoo-ha!" he snapped. "This is a serious matter. How do you lowlifes expect me to perform my duties in the midst of such ridiculousness? Enough!"

Like the mesomorph and his genital, the gentlemen reluctantly obeyed.

Dr. Thunderlove waited for the mesomorph's blood to dry. It took five minutes. While waiting, he told another handful of dirty jokes. They weren't as funny as the jokes he had used to warm up the gentlemen, but they garnered the same pseudoenthusiastic response.

Once the blood had formed into a thin brown crust on his skin, Dr. Thunderlove took a deep breath and flexed his muscles, once, sharply, at maximum intensity. The crust exploded off of his body and flaked to the floor in slow motion...

...return to realtime. His body was perfectly clean and sanitary now. Except for his face, of course—a blood mask with two gigantic round eyes still clung to it. He left it there.

He removed his top hat and flung it aside, exposing a head of slicked-back platinum hair. He readjusted his mustache to make sure it stayed in place.

"Right. Now let's see if we can't turn this heap of useless flesh into a Body without Organs."

"I'm not...useless," bitched the mesomorph.

The bitch was not well received. Growling like a dog whose spine has been stepped on, Dr. Thunderlove plunged into the gaping cavity of the mesomorph and tore out his viscera in an hysterical frenzy. The diegetic reality of the room slipped into fasttime, into slowtime, into fasttime as scintillating vitals were exhumed and disseminated...an emphysemic lung skipped across the crystal floor, wigwagging like a mauled walleye...a kidney exploded in a clenched fist...a cirrhotic liver bounced into a trap door that suddenly appeared, opened, closed, burped, disappeared...unctuous glands, tissue, gristle, phlegm, cartilage, fecal matter, tumbleweed...sound of naked schizos riverdancing in a vat full of wine grapes...a hairy spleen...buckshot veins...squirting pancreatic fluid...a stomach aerated by ulcers sailed to the ceiling and struck a gentlemen in the face, knocking him cold and dreaming...intestines bloomed into the static air in every direction, thick ropes of mucous, a cartoon volcano of gruesome, writhing tendrils...

...freeze-frame...image on the mind's screen of the knocked-out gentleman of a 3D stick figure sprinting across a vast expanse of colorless tundra...

"There's more," whispered the doctor...He thrust his hand into the mesomorph up to the elbow, to the shoulder, rummaging...He pulled out a skeleton. Not the mesomorph's—it was far too small. And not human. He threw it on the floor, stomped on it, screamed at it. He pulled out one, two, three more skeletons and stomped on and screamed at them. Echoic clatter of scattering bones...

Silence.

"This closet is chocked full of dirty little secrets, isn't it?" intoned the doctor.

"Ha-ha-ha-ha-ha-ha-ha-ha-ha-ha-ha-ha-ha-ha-ha-ha," said the gentlemen.

"My body, this paper, this fire," breathed the mesomorph.

Dr. Thunderlove winced. "Paper?" He smiled. "The pathetic delirium of a dead thing, folks. But wait..."

He grabbed the mesomorph. He carefully but assertively opened him wider and stuck his head into the lion's mouth of his rib cage. "Hello!" he bellowed. The word echoed...but not a sufficient number of times. He shook his head madly...and plunged into the mesomorph again, this time with both arms. On occasion he came up for air as he fumbled and groped, cursing in different languages. Finally he pulled out for good. In the firm grip of his fists was a twitching fiberoptic mass. He tossed it over his shoulder, took a step backwards and casually shielded his eyes.

It was as if a sewage pipe had burst deep in the bowels of the mesomorph. There was a low frequency grumbling noise that sharply escalated into a sonic shriek. By degrees the shriek was imitated by the igloo of gentlemen, whose eardrums nearly burst from the hideous force of the hatewave of Sound that seemed to consume them from the inside-out.

The mesomorph's back arched up on the concrete slab as another spectacle of gore erupted out of him. This spectacle did not consist of organs and viscera, but of words and images, thick strips of gelatinous film tape swarming with an impossible datastorm of audiofleshed curses, affirmations, theories, philosophies, colloquialisms, off-the-cuff remarks...Then out poured the hard technology, the steaming detritus of torn apart engines and turbines, machinic claws and pha-langes and chewed-up genitals, a toy robot, a construction beam, metallic shanks, gears, levers, knobs, a geometry of neon wires and wetware, all of it saturated in a blazing cirrus of hot sparks. The last thing to erupt from the mesomorph was a tall, thin brick wall mired in bathroom graffiti. The wall shot into the air, hung there for a moment, and then toppled squarely onto the floor, shattering into thousands of tinkling pieces...

...the smoke cleared.

"Is it over?" said one of the gentlemen, blinking.

Another blinked and said, "My ears hurt."

Another blinked and said, "My soul hurts."

Another blinked and said, "I want my mother."

"That'll do, I think," said Dr. Thunderlove, who stood triumphantly over the deflated body of the mesomorph like a gladiator, his fists clenched, his muscles taut, a bright white rictus grin cutting his blood mask in two. "The autopsy is complete."

Despite their aches and pains, the gentlemen automatically

clicked their tongues. During the applause another trap door opened. A small, gaunt, bent-headed janitor wearing a black-and-white striped jailbird uniform clambered out of it and began to clean up the carnage with an industrial broom...

Once Dr. Thunderlove was finished being proud of himself, he removed the fake mustache from his overlip and flicked it aside. It accidentally struck the janitor in the ear. "Pardon me," said the doctor. The janitor nodded sternly and continued with his business.

The mesomorph lay catatonic on the concrete slab like a used, torn-open tea bag. He stared at the ceiling with glossy, dilated eyes. His grey tongue was sticking out of his mouth, laying as lifelessly on his chin as his terminal genital was laying on his leg. Dr. Thunderlove leaned over him and whispered, "How do you feel, my friend?"

There was a pause before the mesomorph's tongue slowly retracted into his mouth and he gurgled, "I don't know. I...can't tell. I feel dead. I feel...*alive*."

Dr. Thunderlove shook his head. "Dead or alive, only when one has been fully exhumed can one begin to feel anything at all. Do you understand? Now you are finally in a position to produce something. The question is, what will you choose to produce?"

The mesomorph coughed, choked, coughed, coughed...He arched up his head enough to view the ramparts of his hollowed out body. He struggled to push himself onto his elbows. The doctor didn't help him; he observed the struggle with idle curiosity. Once the mesomorph had stabilized himself, he looked into the doctors wide, round eyes. "*Choose* to produce? Choice is a fiction. Whatever I produce will have nothing to do with choice, and everything to do with inevitability."

The doctor shrugged. "Have it your way. But could you move it along please? I'd like to get a workout in before supper. The wife is making my favorite. Finger sandwiches!"

The mesomorph ran the tip of his tongue across his lips: finger sandwiches were his favorite, too. He had to get out of this place...Dizzy, he shifted his weight onto one of his elbows. He used his free hand to reach deep inside of his wound and yank out what resembled a rubber bathtub stopper attached to a length of chain. The room instantly began to quake...

"Shit," said Dr. Thunderlove, and was sucked head-first into the body of the mesomorph. He was followed by the nightstand, the janitor, and all of the viscous material that had been extracted from his body. The gentlemen recommenced shrieking as a potent little squall materialized in the room and broke it down, piece by piece. The gentlemen were torn apart as they imploded into the belly of the mesomorph.

When it was over, the mesomorph carefully tore the flaps of his torso from the nails that bound them and covered up his innards. The flaps came together like pursed lips. They formed a pulsing purple scar, but the scar quickly expired, melting into his flesh...

The mesomorph rolled off of the concrete slab and gently stood erect. It was a struggle: his body, while it looked the same as always, was a heavy burden. Overhead men wearing three-piece suits with antique jetpacks strapped to their backs flowed across the black sky of the city.

Yawning, he began to move across the crystal floor. He took steps that were as ponderous as they were delicate and prudent, waiting for a trap door to appear, and open, and accommodate the extent of his dire immanence...

Protractor Men

They could solve any problem with the use of their protractors. Didn't matter if the problem was an equation, a flat tire, or a world war. As long as their protractors were positioned correctly and the appropriate measure of logic was administered, nothing could stop them.

There was a little boy who had lost a marble in a sewer. Tears rolled down his cheeks as he kneeled over the sewer, staring into its forbidden depths. The protractor men were on their way to lunch when they spotted him. "Step aside, young thing," one of them muttered. They applied and reapplied their protractors to the boy. They applied and reapplied them to the sewer. They huddled up, exchanged a short sequence of hurried whispers, and used mechanical pencils to scribble numbers, signs, chickenscratch, hieroglyphics onto crumpled up pieces of paper. Before the boy could stand up and wipe the tears from his face, he was holding the lost marble in his hand, and the protractor men were cramming through the front door of their favorite deli...

There were two thing-doers flicking one another's noses on a street corner. They were not yelling at or cursing one another, nor did they try to avoid being flicked. Wearing a cold, closed expression, each thing-doer took his turn raising a fist in front of his adversary's nose, holding it there a moment, striking the nose with an index finger catapulted off of an underthumb, carefully retracting the finger back into the fist, and finally allowing the fist to uncurl and fall dead at his side. The protractor men were on their way to get haircuts when they spotted the conflict. "My, how those old noses must sting!" exclaimed one of them. It was true: each nose was bright red and pulsing with pain—evidently the thing-doers had been at it for some time. Not to worry. In a matter of minutes the two combatants were hugging each other and making all kinds of emotionally charged faces as their saviors skillfully shoved their protractors and mechanical pencils back into their holsters and blustered across the street to their favorite barbershop...

There was a mathematician sitting by himself in a café. He was trying to solve a geometrical equation that, once solved, would reveal proof of the existence of God. The protractor men were on their way to the restroom when they spotted him. They didn't bother stopping to give him a helping hand. Not because their bladders were brimming with three quadruple espressos a piece, but because equations weren't worth their time, no, they weren't worth their precious time...

Even matters of the heart were no match for the protractor men. A married couple hated each other and wanted a divorce, a teenage freak was in love with a teenage cheerleader who shuddered at the sight of his zit-stained face, a disgruntled drag queen realized he enjoyed sandwiches more than the company of his lover—it didn't matter how bleak the situation appeared. If the situation crossed their path, the protractor men nipped it in the bud and left nothing but love and devotion in their wake.

Death, too, was perfectly negotiable, although it required more calculations to arbitrate death than it did other inconveniences. The protractor men had spent up to two hours drawing angles and coordinates and equations all over corpses' bodies before the corpses finally opened their eyes and started living again. They tried to stay clear of death, though, worried that PCP would start treating them like messiahs and invading their privacy.

They worried a lot about their fellow PCP, the protractor men. Mostly they worried about the ways PCP might annoy them, which is the primary reason they did what they did: in their eyes, all problems, complicated or elementary, amounted to sheer annoyance, and their primary modus operandi for solving problems was to minimize the degree of annoyance they experienced in their everyday lives. It didn't matter that virtually all of the problems they encountered had nothing to do with them. The very notion of the existence of a problem was annoying. None of the protractor men had jobs, but they always had things to do. All they wanted to do was to be able to execute the things they had to do without being bothered by PCP acting like PCP.

On occasion a protractor man's altruistic gene kicked in. He stood on a wooden shoebox and preached to his colleagues about the moral advantages of good deeds in today's hypermediatized society. Before long the other protractor men were nodding in affirmation, and shortly thereafter their collective problem-solving escapades were administered with an alarming sense of eleemosynary purposefulness. For a few hours, at least. Soon PCP started getting on their nerves again, and they ceased helping them out of goodwill in favor of good riddance.

Perhaps the most distasteful PCP the protractor men were obliged to negotiate were the protractor men themselves. Their existence as organisms who could use protractors to fix anything and everything was annoyingly problematic on a number of social, philosophical, metaphysical and phenomenological levels, not to mention that each protractor man had a hideous ego and a raging solipsistic attitude. It was not uncommon that one of them would sneak up on a colleague as he slept with the intent of negating his existence. Sometimes the effort was successful and the victim would implode, explode, or simply vaporize. But usually the victim would wake up in the middle of being negated and counteract the deed with his own protractor, which almost invariably evolved into a pointless tickle fight that lasted for hours on end.

For the most part, though, the protractor men didn't try to kill themselves. If one of them unnerved another, he would simply wait for an opportune moment to make his watch tell the wrong time, or to render his fly unzipped, or to produce a hairy mole on the tip of his nose, or to turn his shoelaces into strips of corroded bologna, or to turn his penis into an outspoken shrunken head...Tomfoolery of any kind was game. But the game did require a certain amount of touchyfeelyness—no problem could be fixed, no act committed unless a protractor came into physical contact with it—and many of the protractor men lacked stealth and were unable to antagonize their colleagues without being discovered and subsequently ridiculed. So they would have to invent other ways of being annoying, such as whistling off key, or impersonating talk show hosts, or sounding off hogcalls without warning, or telling strangers that they were really a bunch of gay rights activists in disguise...Whatever their limitations, they generally managed to antagonize their colleagues without erasing them from *The Book of Life*. There were only so many protractor men in the world, after all. Even though they more or less despised one another, even though they wanted to curse one another, and to beat one another, and to tear one another to shreds and viscera, they maintained order amongst themselves out of respect for their talent and commonality...

Haberdashery

A customer flowed through the revolving mirror-door, strode over to the nearest salesman and introduced himself. "I am Ashenbach," he said, "but everybody calls me Thunderlove." The salesman returned the greeting, saying, "A pleasure to meet you, Mr. Ashenbach slash Thunderlove. I am a salesman. Everybody calls me a salesman."

"Very well, salesman," said Ashenbach/Thunderlove, and slapped him across the face.

The salesman's head froze in a snapped-back position for a moment, then returned to its normal position. His face was a tightened sphincter. "Thank you, sir," he muttered through clenched teeth. "How may I be of service to you?"

Ashenbach/Thunderlove slapped him across the other cheek. This time the salesman said, "Shit!" He quickly apologized for the expletive and once again asked how he might give his customer a helping hand. Ashenbach/Thunderlove smirked, nodded, and removed his hat. He flicked a piece of lint off of the hat's floppy girth and presented it to the salesman as one might present a slice of vintage cake to a connoisseur of desserts.

"I purchased this hat from this haberdashery," said Ashenbach/Thunderlove.

"Yes," said the salesman.

"It doesn't fit my head."

"I see."

"It's too tight."

"Indeed."

"Additionally, I don't like the looks of this hat. It's ugly."

"Of course it is."

"And it's out of date. Who wears East German fighter pilot hats anymore?"

"Nobody does."

"That's my point."

"Point well taken."

"Is it?"

"Indeed."

"Then please take this abomination away and bring me a hat that is en vogue, handsome, and proportional with my head."

"Right away, sir. I have the perfect thing for you."

"Do you?"

"I do. A special hat for a special customer. Excuse me for a short moment, if you would be so kind, as I retire to The Back Room to do your bidding. Be back in the jiffiest of jiffs." Before retiring to The Back Room, the salesman tentatively presented a cheek to Ashenbach/Thunderlove, but the man declined, opting to nail him in the chin with a powerful undercut. The salesman flew across the haberdashery, arms flailing, and crashed into a stack of empty hat boxes. The other occupants of the haberdashery observed the violence with idle, disinterested eyes, if they bothered to observe it at all. The salesman lay unconscious in the cardboard rubble for thirty seconds before a manager noticed his TKOed, crumpled-up body and revived him with a handful of smelling salts.

The salesman kipped up into a fastwalk, zipped across the hardwood floor, and sprang into an open manhole. Beneath the manhole was the mile-deep spiral staircase that led to The Back Room. The salesman bustled down it as fast as he could...

Ashenbach/Thunderlove folded his arms behind his back and strolled over to the nearest looking glass. Like all of the looking glasses in the shop, it was tall and thin and belonged in a funhouse: it distorted the image of every man it reflected, imploring every man that looked at it to make distorted faces and adopt a distorted stance so as to produce a clear image of himself. Ashenbach/Thunderlove, however, had little interest in the appearance of his reflection. He stood tall in front of the looking glass, staring at himself with a straight body and a blank face. He removed a giant comb from the inner jacket pocket of his goodbody suit and began to restyle his Figaro hairdo with slow, swooping, calculated strokes.

As he attended to the hairdo, he eavesdropped on select conversations-in-progress between other customers and salesmen. The penalty for eavesdropping in Pseudofolliculitis City, depending upon who is playing judge on the day of sentencing, ranges from indefinite incarceration, to public beheading, to MR. D. (Maximum Risk Defenestration), to mere name-calling. But the minions of The Law treated the insurrection as halfheartedly as they treated things like loitering, jaywalking, evil-eyeing, and farting out loud, and at any rate Ashenbach/Thunderlove was a friend of the grandson of

Pseudofolliculitis City's founder. If he wanted, he could walk into a police station, moon everybody in sight, and get off scot-free...

...The customer had unbuttoned the top three buttons of his dress shirt and exposed a hairy chest. The salesman was scrutinizing the chest with wide, round eyes. His sharp lips stuck out as if pinched by a clothespin. "Hmm," he kept saying.

The customer's chin was resting on his clavicle bone. He was squinting at his chest. His lips were puckered into a white ring of flesh. "Do you see any yet?" he kept saying.

Eventually the salesman replied, "I think I might. I think I might." Then: "No. False alarm. My apologies, sir."

"Come closer. Here. Right here." The customer pointed at a patch of hair located above his left nipple. "See?"

Keeping his feet planted, the salesman leaned closer and adjusted the pince-nez perched on the tip of his beaklike nose.

"Now do you see it?"

"Yes, sir," the salesman lied.

The customer said, "Really? Because I don't see anything. I was just pointing at my chest arbitrarily. My wife says the hairs in my chest are losing their pigment, but I don't see any lack of pigment in any of these damned hairs. Are you sure?"

"Not *quite* sure, sir," the salesman lied. Now he actually thought he saw a colorless hair. "No, not quite sure."

"What will I do without my pigment?" the customer asked in the sad voice of a child.

The salesman stood up straight and removed his pince-nez. He sighed. "I don't know, sir. Perhaps a new hat will take your mind off the matter. Might I interest you in the latest model of fedora? We call it the Van Kleef. Right this way please." With a sweep of his arm, he motioned the customer in the appropriate direction.

The customer didn't budge. He had slipped into a powerful depression; for the moment, he no longer existed in the real world. He stood before the salesman with a bent head and hunched over shoulders. On his face he wore a mask of sheer melancholy. A bead of drool was making its way out of the corner of the mask's mouth.

"My pigment," he whispered...

...and zipped up his pants.

"I see," said the salesman, nervously glancing around the haberdashery for the manager. The customer dealt him a grinning nod, then abruptly broke out into "The Sound of Music." He sang the song at the top of his lungs in a quicksilver alto.

"Please, sir," the salesman implored. "Please don't do that. The manager...ahem, he doesn't like it when customers do things like that."

The customer instantly clammed up. He made an I-have-an-entire-lime-wedged-inside-my-mouth face.

"The customer is always right," he said sharply, and kneed the salesman in the groin. The salesman doubled over, grabbed his genitals. He hopped up and down until the pain subsided and he was able to stand erect. "That's true," he replied. "But what is true is *never* what is acknowledged as being true."

The customer unzipped his pants again. This time he let them fall to his ankles. He wasn't wearing any underwear. He used the dunce cap the salesman had been trying to sell him as a toilet. The salesman observed the spectacle of defecation with cool resolution. When he was finished, the customer handed the cap to the salesman and said, "That's true. But the truth that the truth is never acknowledged as being true is itself never acknowledged as being true. Not in decent society anyway. What is this noise? Isn't this supposed to be a five star haberdashery?"

The salesman muttered inarticulately as the customer pulled his pants up and slipped on a pair of brass knuckles...

At the same time another customer was calmly, systematically slapping another salesman across the face with a long-fingered leather glove. Both men's chins were slightly upturned, and their aloof yet self-righteous expressions belonged to the corporate figureheads of Uppity Sass Industries. The customer took turns on the salesman's cheeks, pausing for a few seconds between slaps. He didn't slap him hard enough to make him wince or swear out loud. But it was hard enough to induce a certain amount of restrained jaw-flexing. Not a word leaked out of the bushy handlebar mustaches that concealed the two men's lipless mouths.

A large rack of sombreros and ten gallon hats was accidentally tipped over by a customer's son. There was a crash, a pause, a shriek. The shriek didn't come out of the son's mouth as his father spanked him with a portable two-by-four, it came out of the manager's mouth as the hats fell down and flooded the floor.

The blank-faced son blinked as his wild-eyed father wailed on his ass.

Paying no attention, a salesman overturned the fez he was holding. Nothing came out. He flicked the fez with his finger. Nothing came out. He hammered the fez with his fist.

The vermin fell out and landed on its back with a pained squeak. Its legs flailed in the air as it struggled to right itself and scuttle away.

A customer said, "Earlier today there was a fly in my soup. Now this?"

"Not at all, sir," smiled the salesman. "This is one of our premier products, in fact, on special for just eighty-nine doll hairs."

"That's a lot of doll hairs for a special. I don't see what's so special about it."

The salesman lifted his hand, closed his eyes, and turned his head to one side. "Observe, sir." He opened his eyes, fixed them on the vermin, and folded his arms across his chest. He paused. The customer pushed out his lips. The vermin flailed.

The salesman lifted up his leg and stomped on the vermin with all of his might.

"Jesus," said the customer. He said "Jesus" again when the salesman lifted up his wingtip and revealed a perfectly healthy, perfectly alive vermin. Unharmed by the vicious stomp, it continued to struggle to flip itself upright.

"That's not the long and short of it either," remarked the salesman proudly. "You can stomp on this bastard all you want and the sonuvabitch won't die! Watch!" He stomped on the vermin ten times in quick, robotic succession. As promised, the vermin abided. The salesman dealt the customer a giant plastic grin. "You can't get a better deal than that, comrade. Not in this town. Think about it: an indestructible vermin! And a fez to keep it safe in."

The customer cocked his head. "You do have a point. Tell you what, I'll give you fifty for it. How would that be?"

The salesman winced. "This is not a pawn shop, sir. This is a reputable haberdashery. Please don't insult me. I am just a salesman and you may slap me across the face at your leisure, but please don't insult me. Eighty-nine doll hairs—take it or leave it."

The customer frowned. He fingered his chin. He gestured with his lips. He glanced down at the vermin and observed its adamant struggle.

A large shitkicker infiltrated the customer's line of vision and fell on the vermin like an anvil. Blood and guts splashed out of either side of the shitkicker's sole as the vermin exploded like a piece of ripe fruit.

"Jesus."

Startled, the salesman nearly leapt out of his pants. "How dare your, sir!" he barked. "Who do you think you are?"

"I am Ashenbach," said the man, giving the salesman a proverbial slap, "but everybody calls me Thunderlove." He lifted up his shitkicker. The smashed remains of the vermin oozed gore. A few of its extremities convulsed.

The salesman had not been prepared for the slap, which sent him spinning around like a top. He fell down and passed out from dizziness, woke up, stood up, shook the butterflies out of his head. "Pardon me, my good man," he wheezed. "My mistake. But I am only obliged to wait on one customer at a time. Have you not been helped? Additionally, I would prefer it if you didn't stomp on any merchandise until you have purchased it. Indulge me in that capacity if you will."

"This is false advertising," the customer broke in. "You told me that vermin was indestructible. You told me it wouldn't die. Well, it's roadkill. This is some scam you're running."

Ashenbach/Thunderlove stared at the salesman.

The salesman bunched up his face. "Why are you harassing me and my customer? Is somebody assisting you? Somebody will be with you momentarily. Somebody will—"

Ashenbach/Thunderlove nailed him in the windpipe with the blade of his hand.

The salesman's eyeballs ballooned out of his head as he clutched his neck, gasped, and coughed blood up onto his bleached white major domo uniform. Once he was able to breathe again, Ashenbach/Thunderlove replied, "I'm being waited on by somebody. Somebody has been waiting on me for quite some time now. I'm bored. I don't like being bored. I have ants in my pants, you see. You see?" He unbuckled his belt and pulled his trousers down over his hip. Sure enough, there was a constellation of ants tearing across his flesh in a confused frenzy. He pulled his trousers up, buckled his belt. "Needless to say, it's difficult for me to stay still for more than a few seconds at a time. And when I overheard you trying to sell this man something that doesn't exist, well—"

"Eavesdropper!" the salesman interjected. After receiving a backhand, one from each customer, he sputtered, "Excuse me, friends. I don't know what came over me. The way in which a follicle breaks The Law is nobody's business but his own. Apologies, apologies. Now then. Who is your salesman, Mr. Ashenbach slash Thunderlove?"

"I'm not sure. He looked exactly like you, and he called himself a salesman. Then he retired to The Back Room to get me a new hat, one that befits me. He's been gone for a half hour."

"The Back Room!" the salesman cried. "Well, that explains it. The Back Room is not an easy place to achieve. One must make a considerable journey to get there. But it's worth it. The Back Room is nothing less than a Valhalla of hats—only the best and the brightest, it contains. We ask you to be patient, Mr. Ashenbach slash Thunderlove. No doubt it will pay off in the end. A man without a befitting hat, after all, is not a real man. Everything is going to be all right."

But everything was not all right. Twenty minutes ago the salesman who had been attending to Ashenbach/Thunderlove had tripped on the spiral staircase that led down to The Back Room, despite the class he had taken in Stairway Walking while working on his M.A.* He had been a quarter of a mile down the staircase at the time and fell end over end the remaining three quarters of a mile. He died from a blow to the head half a mile away from the bottom. Now he lay dead at the foot of the stairway, which coiled up into the distance behind him. In front of him was a giant wooden door with a giant neon sign on it that read:

THE BACK ROOM!

The Back Room was as large as Spacetime Square and as empty as The Museum of Deep Meaning. It was entirely devoid of follicles. It was devoid of all life forms except for the gargantuan creature loafing in the middle of its vast expanse. The creature was the size of a dinosaur and resembled a praying mantis that has had all of its limbs ripped off, except for its head, which was a replica of the head of The Founder of Pseudofolliculitis City, handlebar mustache and all. Growing out of the head was a tall stovepipe hat dripping with mucous and smoldering with smoke. Its blind eyes were the color of stale milk.

The creature spoke in half-hearted Pentecostal tongues as it lounged on the crystal floor of The Back Room, twitching in subdued agony.

Its tail was a great colonic appendage that, like its hat, dripped mucous and smoldered smoke. The tip of the tail was a gaping fishlike

---

*Master's degree in Asskissing. All of the salesmen that work in the haberdashery are lawfully required to hold a M.A. Moreover, anybody who attempts to apply for the position of salesman at the haberdashery without a M.A. in his possession must endure a three stage punishment that consists of the following: 1) a long-winded invective during which the subject is irrationally screamed at and belittled; 2) a spanking machine constructed out of no less than fifteen human bodies; 3) the plucking of one eyebrow, hair by hair. The order in which this punishment is executed varies.

mouth. For the most part it lay still. Every twelve hours, when the massive clock face that constituted the ceiling of The Back Room struck its mark, the tail would leap to attention, writhe and gesticulate, burp and pardon itself, and finally spit out a newborn hat. Then it would carefully pick the hat up and deposit it on one of the thousands of shelves that constituted the walls of The Back Room.

One of these hats would have belonged to Ashenbach/Thunderlove. Tando hat #6491D, if the salesman that had been attending to him would have had his way. But by the time the corpse of the salesman was discovered, and by the time a surrogate salesman was ordered to take his place and wait on his customer, Ashenbach/Thunderlove had already sequestered his lawyer and established a strong case against the haberdashery.

The Personalities

A PCP bought a box of new personalities and rented an audience to test them out. He wanted to see how they might work in the real world before actually trying them out in the real world. He was a very fastidious PCP. The audience consisted of actors that had not performed a sufficient number of oral sex acts on a sufficient number of motion picture executives to earn their Guild cards. Each of the actors was to be paid the standard salary for a day's worth of extra work.

There were four personalities inside the box. The PCP opened it up, removed one of the personalities, and put it on.

"Well?" he said, glaring at the audience. "Do your jobs and react to me, goddamn it. My personality is the cause—*you* are my effect."

The actors blinked at him. They were sitting in a half-circle of aluminum fold-out chairs. All of their backs were stiff, all of their hands were resting palm-down on their knees.

Must be a dud, thought the PCP. He took off the personality, tossed it onto the floor, stomped on it, removed another personality from the box, and put it on.

The actors blinked at him. One of them coughed. Another sniffed.

"Ah-ha," said the PCP, and raised an eyebrow. An actor copied him and raised his eyebrow. Another actor copied the actor that was copying the PCP and raised his eyebrow. Another actor copied that actor, and another actor copied that actor, and another one copied another one, and so on until all of the actors' faces possessed one raised eyebrow.

The PCP studied the audience for a moment, gauging and judging their quixotic behavior. "Interesting," he said. "*Very* interesting. But not my style, I'm afraid." He ripped off the personality and flung it into an open manhole somebody had engraved into a nearby wall.

He put on a third personality.

The audience immediately burst into applause. It took no time at all for the PCP to read into this piece of reflexivity. "That's *definitely* not my style," he snorted, taking off the personality and throwing it at one of the actors. The personality attached itself to the actor's head like a baby squid. His colleagues promptly turned to him and pointed their applause in his direction. The actor stood up and took a garish bow before removing the personality from himself and inducing dead silence.

"Why do follicles clap, for godsakes?" said the PCP as he slipped on the fourth and last personality. "You wanna make some noise, open your mouth and bark at the moon."

A handful of actors followed the PCP's orders, tilted up their chins and began to bark. The other actors all made constipated faces. Except for one of them. One of them farted, as if in response to the offensive character of the constipated faces, and then made a calm, cool, collected face of his own.

The PCP nodded. He said, "I see," and studied the codings of the audience's conduct. He scratched his nose, twitched his lips. "Hmm," he mused. "Hmm. Hmm. Hmm." Suspicion overwhelmed him. Were the audience's reactions to his personalities genuinely, authentically reactionary? Or were they staged? The audience was a bunch of actors, after all. Granted, the PCP was the one who had hired the actors, and so, if they were being true to their false nature, he was ultimately the one to blame. But he had still paid them all to react to him, and he expected them to act like professionals; if they weren't behaving truthfully, they should at least be acting like they were behaving truthfully, that is, they should be acting like they weren't acting. But maybe they *were* acting like they weren't acting. The PCP couldn't tell.

"You weirdos better not be messing with my head," he carped. "I'm paying you good money to do the right thing. Well, maybe not good money, but money. Understand?"

The audience stared at the PCP.

The PCP closed his eyes and shook his head, realizing there was no way he would ever be able to tell if the actors were being sincere. And in any case he had run out of new personalities to try on. He paid them in cashier's checks and said they could go. The actors thanked him one at a time, shook his hand one at a time…took their personalities off one at a time. The PCP frowned. His frowned deepened as the actors continued to take off their personalities until all that was left of them was an assembly of dark, featureless stick figures.

The PCP placed his hands on his hips and said, "I said *I* was the cause. I said *you* were the effect."

In response, the stick figures posed and froze like mimes…

The Other Pedestrian

Somebody let the roosters out of their cages. They're running all over the city going "Cock-a-doodle-do!"...

Pedestrians pushed out their lips and observed the frenzy with eyes like wet blueberries. One of them said, "Look at those old roosters! I once had an uncle who was a rooster. No kidding. He used to go like this!" Crouching down on his knees, he flapped his elbows and pecked his nose into the sidewalk to prove to the pedestrian standing next to him that he was telling the truth.

The other pedestrian blinked. He pulled a fistful of corn out of his pocket and sprinkled it onto the ground.

The pedestrian squawked. He excitedly pecked it up.

"Good boy," said the other pedestrian. He pulled out and disbursed another fistful of corn.

Again the pedestrian squawked and excitedly pecked it up.

The other pedestrian made a frog face. Realizing he was out of eats, he told the pedestrian to keep an eye on his briefcase, excused himself, and hurried to a nearby feed store. Meanwhile, the pedestrian strutted up and down on the sidewalk, snapping at the occasional passerby...

The other pedestrian returned with a ten pound burlap bag of corn slung over his shoulder. "I'm back!" he exclaimed. He tore the bag open, fed the pedestrian until he was fat enough to slaughter, pulled a machete out of his briefcase, cut off his head, dragged the corpse by the heel to a nearby butcher's shop, and traded it for half a pound of tightly wrapped, thinly sliced honey turkey.

Meanwhile, the roosters are running all over the city going "Cock-a-doodle-do!"...

PCP

Pseudofolliculitis City has a tendency to induce phobias in its inhabitants. In light of the vast number of conceivable persecutors that live and lurk in PC, these phobias are occasionally linked to some form of paranoia. But for the most part they operate according to their own irrational logic.

All legal PCP have a phobia. Not just a whimsical fear of an object or stimulus, but a potent, affective fear that intervenes with and redirects the operations of their daily life. It is a pre-wreck for all PCP, the same as tax-paying and hat-wearing are pre-wrecks, and if one is not genetically inclined to be acutely afraid of something, a phobia is surgically inscribed onto the fabric of one's psyche. The Law decrees it, and everybody agrees with it, knowing that the social body cannot exist in a functional manner without a healthy injection of freakery animating its flesh and bone.

Tourists of PC—if you're interested in knowing more about this curious affliction, all you have to do is approach a PCP, tap it on the shoulder, and ask what ails it. As long as it is not in the process of negotiating the pangs of its phobia, you may find it quite friendly and willing to externalize itself. But this is a rarity. There is also the drawback that you might tap the shoulder of an ickylophobe in whose case you would function as the catalyst of the phobic pang. Ickylophobes are not only afraid of tourists, they have a moral objection to you; as they see it, there is no rational excuse for leaving the place you live in. Anybody who does leave is irrational and deranged and worthy of an unsportsmanlike asskicking. Most ickylophobes maintain a strict diet of Colby cheese and iceberg lettuce, however, and are usually too scrawny and feeble to execute an asskicking. But they will try. In order to avoid a potentially embarrassing public skirmish, use caution when you select a PCP to interrogate, and stay clear of all bodies distinguished by emaciation.

You will want to stay clear of bodies distinguished by corpulence, too. They are generally not of good cheer. Once a PCP surpasses a certain weight, it is arrested and sentenced to cacomorphobia (fear of fat follicles). As further punishment, it is denied the right to lose weight for a period of no less than five years; any attempt to do so and it is literally served the death penalty, which entails being force-fed an immoderate portion of fast food products. The cacomorphobe's affliction is almost as dire as the pantophobe's, whose fear of fear itself garners the most unpredictable behavior of any PCP. Unfortunately pantophobes cannot be identified by their external image.

PC is not a place for the socially squeamish. If you have difficulty being near or interacting with organisms that do not possess the ability to comport themselves in a conventionally civilized manner, do not set foot on the ferroconcrete of this urban dreamscape. Behind every pair of eyes you see lurks a strange and unusual cognitive tsunami. Stroll down the slidewalks and jetpack the skyways at your own risk. Every PCP is an accident waiting to happen. Look to your left, point to your right, throw a dart out the window and you will no doubt strike a follicle beset with ataxophobia (fear of disorder or untidiness), or trichophobia (fear of hair), or samhainophobia (fear of Halloween), or ergophobia (fear of work), or leukophobia (fear of the color white), or clinophobia (fear of beds), or epistaxiophobia (fear of nosebleeds), or katagelophobia (fear of being ridiculed), or iophobia (fear of poison), or ombrophobia (fear of rain), or sophophobia (fear of learning), or chronomentrophobia (fear of clocks) ...

One PCP your dart will not strike is the ochlophobe. Fear of crowds prohibits it from leaving its apartment, where it lives out its days in a lonely but not necessarily unhappy fashion. It has all of life's necessities delivered to it at home and usually makes its living jacked into the Schizoverse, peddling pseudodesigner products to virtual selves who are either ugly or possess inferior hairlines and genitals (strangely, virtual crowds don't invoke The Fear). Based on the findings of a recent survey, its favorite pastime is taking naps. Second is cow tipping, a feat that, for obvious reasons, must be accomplished by means of daydreaming. Customarily ochlophobes are sedentary and do not make a habit out of bodily movement. But sometimes they will leap out of their seats like cats whose tails have been stepped on and start doing jumping jacks. On occasion they will strip naked, spray Stick Em all over their bodies and crawl across the walls and ceilings of their apartments, pretending to be insects—their third favorite pastime, incidentally.

This comment from a loitering PCP with verbophobia (fear of words) who tentatively speaks into The Author's microphone: "Good thing those...ochlophobes ain't no...nudiphobes, too!...Otherwise th-th-they wouldn't be able t-t-t-to...take the-their...clothes...off and...Ahhhhhh!" Unable to bear the substance coming out of his mouth, he throws his arms over his head and runs away, knocking speedwalkers over like bowling pins.

Coincidentally there is a masochistic PCP with hippopotomonstrosesquippedaliophobia (fear of long words) curled up in an alleyway across the street. He has been whispering "Antidisestablishmentarianism" to himself over and over for two days now, experiencing up to one orgasm every three hours as a result of The Pain ...

PAN DOWN the street three blocks. FREEZE-FRAME at the front door of The Lobster Pot fish n' chips shop where a trichophobic (afraid of hair) street preacher is shaving his already smooth, bald head with a gigantic Rambo knife while giving a sermon about the evils of not being hadephobic (afraid of hell) and being ecclesiophobic (afraid of church) to a twitching group of homilophobic (afraid of sermons) potato-eaters. PAN UP 544 stories and ZOOM INTO Office #544-239v. Here is another hippopotomonstrosesquippedaliophobe sporting a short-sleeved button-down, a clip-on tie, a mustache that looks like a large ink blot, and a small pot belly. He is standing behind a podium that is too large for him; it rises above his chin so that his pursed mouth is barely visible to the roundtable of PCP that are listening to his speech. Each of these PCP looks like the hippopotomonstrosesquippedaliophobe, give or take a mustache and a pot belly or two. The hippopotomonstrosesquippedaliophobe's affliction is serious. Five letter words are enough to leave a bad taste in his mouth. Words consisting of over ten letters, heard or spoken, invariably produce a fainting spell. So he chooses each word with extreme care, speaking slowly, in a tremulous, mousy voice. For the most part the roundtablers respect his phobia. Every now and then, however, one of them will shout out "Pandiculation!" or "Ultracrepidarian!" or "Honorificabilitudinitatibus!" if only to break the monotony of the subject being addressed. In response, the hippotomonstros-esquippedaliophobe will place the back of his hand on his head and fall over backwards with a whimper.

Such displays of tomfoolery are limited to the private sector. In public, it is a violation of The Law to provoke a PCP by activating its phobia. The penalty for such an offense varies. To play a flute in the presence of an aulophobe, for instance, is a misdemeanor that usually results in a small fine. The same goes for deliberately thumbing through your wallet in the presence of a chrematophobe and pretending you are a pig in the presence of an swinophobe. To capture and imprison an amaxophobe in a carriage, on the other hand, is a felony that can result in imprisonment, as can shoving a swarming beehive onto an apiphobe's head, forcing a belonephobe to walk across pins and needles, and placing a Dutchman within ten feet of a Dutchphobe. The only insurrection of this kind that warrants the death penalty is getting a coulrophobe drunk and unconscious and then painting its face and dressing it up like a clown. Of course, all of these punishments are contingent upon getting caught by one or more of The Law's minions, all of which have their own phobias to contend with and are generally preoccupied. Still, there is a surprising lack of phobic antagonism in the public sector. If you are a PCP, you are typically free to mingle with your fellow follicles without having to worry about them invoking unwanted nastiness. The only thing you are not free from is the unwanted nastiness you invoke in yourself.

Whereas they are not discouraged from visiting PC, tourists are not encouraged to visit it either. True, the city is fraught with spectacles the likes of which the real world has never seen or experienced. But what price are you willing to pay to see and experience them? It is a singular occasion on which a foreign species invades this place without it turning out badly—for the foreigner as much as for the good people of PC. You would do well to mind your own business, if for nothing else than the possibility that, during your stay, you may contract a nasty case of oicophobia (fear of returning home) ...

The Snore

The sleeper woke up to the sound of a powerful snore!

It was coming out of his mouth. The sleeper had never been prone to snoring before. Not even the odd snort or whistle had plagued his unconscious body.

He glanced down at his mouth to make sure a snore was actually coming out of it. There was.

A worried shiver flowed up the sleeper's spine. Was this really happening? Or was he dreaming? He was probably dreaming. But there was no way to tell for sure. He decided to ignore the snore.

He closed his eyes and pretended to have a dream about a sleeper who woke up to the sound of a powerful snore coming out of his mouth. Not being a snorer, the sleeper in this make-believe dream peered down at the snore in disbelief. His eyeballs broke out into a cold sweat. He got out of bed and shuffled into the bathroom. Urinated. Flushed the toilet, flexed his jaw. Looked in the mirror. There was a snore in his mouth all right. It looked like a Chia pet. He tried to spit it out of his mouth, but the snore was incorrigible and wouldn't allow itself to be discharged. He stuck his finger down his throat in an attempt to induce a vomit that would rush up his throat and push the snore out of him. That didn't work either—the moment his finger entered his mouth, the snore bit it off like a stick of beef jerky. The sleeper twitched. He tried to curse as he wrapped a bandage around his bleeding hand, but the snore was so loud his voice was inaudible.

He decided to go back to bed, lay down, and ignore the snore. He closed his eyes and pretended to have a dream about a sleeper who was pretending to have a dream about a sleeper who woke up to the sound of a powerful snore coming out of his mouth. But there was no snore in his mouth. There was a Chia pet, and angry green sprouts were growing out of its body in fasttime...

A knock struck the sleeper's front door. It wasn't a loud knock. It wasn't a soft one either.

The sleeper got out of bed and spit the Chia pet into a garbage can. He smacked his lips as he walked down the hallway towards the front door, trying to get the taste of vegetation out of his mouth.

He glanced through the peephole. Saw nothing. Said, "It's the middle of the night. If you're a thief, go away. If you're a murderer, go away. If you're none of the above, go away. OK?"

The response was a solid, sonorous knock. The sleeper sighed and impatiently opened the door.

"Good evening, sir," said the snore. It was wearing a long black cape, a black stovepipe hat, and sleek-looking mirrorshades.

"*You,*" intoned the sleeper. "What do you want?"

"I was informed of a disturbance at this residence."

"Disturbance? What disturbance?"

The snore smirked. "The absence of me. Which disturbs me."

The sleeper grimaced. "But I don't snore!"

"But you do snore," said the snore.

The sleeper slammed the door. He turned and started back down the hallway.

The door exploded as the snore burst through it like an incensed bull. Splinters of oak leapt onto the ceiling and walls in slow motion...

The sleeper turned around just as the snore fell on him. It threw an elbow into his face. Blood sprayed out of his mouth in slow motion as his head snapped over his shoulder. His vision faded out...faded back in. The snore nodded at him, grinned at him. The sleeper nodded and grinned back...then kicked the snore in the groin. The snore doubled over...then sprung up and chopped the sleeper in the throat. The sleeper coughed, wheezed...rallied and retaliated. In seconds the two of them were engaged in a full-fledged kung fu fight. The fight lasted until morning. Reality slipped in and out of slow motion and fasttime, and digitized techno music poured out of unseen surround-sound speakers. The melody of the music perfectly reflected the ebb and flow of the skirmish.

Both the snore and the sleeper fought well, but in the end the snore won. The sleeper lay on the floor of the hallway in a daze. His eyes were two swollen slits, and his halfway open mouth looked like it had been carved onto his face with a dull razorblade. The snore nodded. It removed its cape and hat and mirrorshades, exposing the sleeper to its grave nakedness. Then it swan dove into the sleeper's grisly mouth.

Later, the sleeper woke up to the sound of a powerful snore...

The Kitchen
a.k.a.
Death of a Salesman II

There was a kitchen growing out of a salesman's back. Cupboards, counters, appliances, a stainless steel sink—the whole shebang. It grew there one night while he was dreaming of mushroom omelets. In the dream he had been cooking four of them simultaneously when the omelets leaped out of their pans and began to dance around the stove's foremost grill without the slightest provocation...

He had tried to purge the kitchen from himself by shaving it, waxing it, electrolysizing it, but nothing worked. Every time he got rid of it, it grew back faster, with larger appliances and more counter space.

It was getting so he couldn't call on his customers in person anymore. Every time he left the house, PCP would sneak up on him and try to raid his refrigerator or cook pasta on his stove. Staying at home wasn't much better. The kitchen there was small and rundown. His wife preferred to use the kitchen on his back, claiming, "If you'd bring home the bacon, I wouldn't have to fry it on your backside." It was true. He was a lousy salesman, and he had no choice but to allow his wife to use him to prepare meals at her leisure.

As punishment for being lousy, his wife cooked the same meal every meal: Chicken Cordon Blah.

"We're sick of eating the same old cowshit!" hollered the salesman's three small children. Lack of diversity had elicited dirty mouths in them. It had also elicited a metabolic change: except for variations in height, each child now resembled a miniature, deflated version of Winston Churchill, complete with bald head, monocle and smoldering cigar.

Something had to be done. Not only was the kitchen jeopardizing the functionality of his profession and the well-being of his family, it was giving him scoliosis.

He decided to jump off of a building.

Before climbing to its roof, he visited his family and said, "Goodbye, folks. I hate you." He also visited his boss and said, "Goodbye, sir. I hate you."

Later, as he stood on the roof's ledge, he said, "Goodbye, self. I hate you, too. I liked you once. Before you became...impure."

Despite the heavy weight of the kitchen on his back, he was able to lift a stiff leg into the air and hold it there for a moment before tipping forward like a toy soldier that's been flicked in the back of the head.

Nothing exited his open mouth as he fell face first into the sidewalk. Not a word, not a scream, not a flailing tongue...

His body broke on impact, shattering to pieces as if made of glass. It also broke the fall of the kitchen, which landed sunny side up. The cupboard door beneath the sink splintered, a few wine glasses cracked, the refrigerator light burst, but for the most part it was all right. The onlookers who had observed the salesman's suicide smiled at this piece of good fortune, and they were careful not step on the pieces of the salesman as they lined up in front of the kitchen, waiting patiently for their turn to prepare a meal at their leisure...

When the Law Has Spoken

The Dimplechins weren't in a good mood. They already owned two vacuum cleaners, one upright and one canister, and both of them worked fine. But Mr. Terminal had endowed Mr. and Mrs. Dimplechin with a particularly seductive brand of sweettalk, and now he was standing in the middle of their living room. Four perturbed faces stared at him from a long, flat couch.

Mr. Dimplechin was a stubby man with a stubby man's complex— the presence of tall, thin follicles like this vacuum cleaner salesman stirred up his insecurities. His striking blue eyes, healthy-looking olive skin, and full head of black hair compensated for his lack of stature to some degree, but not to a degree that made him comfortable with his own image. Not even remotely.

Mrs. Dimplechin was attractive for her age. She had liver spots on her arms and a wrinkled neck, but her mouth was full and supple, and she had a voluptuous hourglass figure. Together with her painted up face—mascara caked around the eyes, blush caked onto the cheeks, dark lipstick caked onto that mouth—these features gave her the air of a retired pornstar.

There were two Dimplechin children, a 13-year-old boy named

Devon and a 16-year-old girl named Doris. Devon was a nerdy bastard; his black helmet of hair seemed to have been grafted onto his head, his big thick glasses were at least three decades out of vogue, and he had these chunky love handles hanging over either side of his skintight Spangler jeans. Doris, on the other hand, was anything but nerdy. She had skin like her father's, smooth and dark, and breasts like her mother's, big and firm. The tight halfshirt she was wearing left her navel exposed. The navel was encircled by a ring of tiny scatological tattoos. A snake tongue had been implanted into her belly button. For the most part the tongue hung motionless against her abdomen, but sometimes it leapt up and emitted a dull hiss. Mr. Terminal glanced at the little spectacle more than once on the sly. Doris had long blond hair. On her face she wore a mask of bitchy teenage angst.

That all of the Dimplechins had tiny dimples in their chins was pure coincidence.

"What the hell is this?" mumbled Doris just as Mr. Terminal was about to throw his pitch. "Who is this asshole?" She glanced back and forth between her parents and the vacuum cleaner salesman.

"Watch your mouth, young lady," growled Mrs. Dimplechin, and shook a finger at her. "Just sit there like a good teenager and keep your hole closed."

Ignoring her mother, Doris looked at her father. "Dad?"

"Fight that adolescence," said Mr. Dimplechin in a dry monotone without looking at her.

Disgusted, Doris slumped back in her seat and violently crossed her arms over her bust. Her belly button gurgled as the tongue in it gesticulated. She was sitting on the end of the couch next to her mother, and her brother was sitting on the other end of the couch next to her father. She stared at Mr. Terminal as if he had killed her best friend.

Mr. Terminal swallowed. He was a well-built, nice-looking follicle with dark features and exceptional mental stamina. Usually nothing daunted him, but he was a little apprehensive now. Not because the Dimplechins were less than enthusiastic about him being there—he had sold the shit out of families with twice the reserved hostility that this one was dishing out—but because his boss was evaluating him. Once a year all vacuum cleaner salesmen that worked for Daddy-O & Sonz had to wear a wire to one of their clients' residences for observation to make sure that they were comporting themselves in a sufficiently civil yet slick and salesworthy manner. Additionally, if a salesman did not close a deal on an occasion during which he was being monitored, he was fired point blank, no questions asked. Mr. Terminal had been with the company for over ten years now and had never failed to produce in the past. But that didn't mean anything. Even if he had been with the company for fifty years, he would be fired if he failed to produce on this day, at this moment.

The wire he was wearing had been taped to his chest. In his ear was a tiny microphone through which his boss could talk to him.

"Don't fuck up," his boss said as he was gearing up to make his pitch. Following the directive was an evil little snicker.

Mr. Terminal flexed his jaw.

"Can we get this bullshit going," blurted Mr. Dimplechin. "We've been sitting here for almost ten seconds now and you haven't said a damned thing. You're just standing there like a damned idiot."

Mr. Terminal raised an eyebrow. Young Devon had just stuck his finger into one of his ears, pulled it out, and was now sniffing it like some flower. Coated in yellow ear wax, the finger glistened in the bright light of the living room. Mr. Terminal felt a pang of nausea in his stomach.

"Get that finger away from your nose!" bleated Mrs. Dimplechin when she got a load of her son. "Jesus. Can't you at least *try* not to be a repugnant little loser?" Devon ignored her and continued to sniff his finger. His mother slapped his hand away from his face. The hand snapped right back. Devon's nose was sniffing furiously now. His mother made a fist, raised it above her head, and came down on his knee like a guillotine. Devon squawked and doubled over. He whimpered as he massaged his hurt knee.

Trying his best to ignore the dysfunctional goings-on of the Dimplechin family, Mr. Terminal forced a smile onto his face. This was it. Time to lay it on them. He couldn't let things unfold in this way anymore. He had to take control of the situation. He had to contain it. If he stood here for much longer without his mouth running, who knows what would happen? At this rate the Dimplechins would be tearing each other apart in a matter of minutes.

The moment before Mr. Terminal was about to start his mouth running, Mr. Dimplechin, who had been fingering the dimple in his chin for that last half minute out of boredom, lost his patience. "Fuck it," he said. "If you're just going to stand there like a dumbass and not say anything, I'm reading the paper. Lemme know when you're gone." He snatched up the newspaper sitting on the coffee table. He opened it up in front of him and disappeared behind its vast wingspan.

"Don't be that way," said Mrs. Dimplechin. She poked her husband with one of her long, fake fingernails. Keeping the paper in front of him, he told her he would murder her if she did that again. Mrs. Dimplechin shook her head. "I'm sorry," she said to Mr. Terminal. "He had a hernia removed a few months ago and he's been unhappy ever since."

She frowned, glanced at the ceiling. "Actually that's not true. Well, it's true, but not entirely. I mean, his unhappiness isn't totally a result of the hernia operation. The thing is, he's been unhappy his whole life."

"I was happy as a child, one day," droned Mr. Dimplechin from behind the paper. "I remember there was one day I felt very good. I forget what I was doing, probably nothing, probably dicking around in the back yard or something, but I'm telling you, I was a happy asshole that day. So don't go spreading rumors about me being unhappy my whole life. Bitch."

Mrs. Dimplechin rolled her eyes. She puffed out her cheeks. "Excuse me for a second, Mr. Terminal. I'll see if I can talk some sense into him. Be right back." She crawled onto her husband's lap and vanished behind the newspaper.

"Fuck's going on over there?" griped the voice of Mr. Terminal's boss. "Are you gonna sell these assholes a vacuum cleaner or what? Make Daddy-O proud!"

Mr. Terminal was now staring at a giant, wide-open newspaper with two cantankerous children sitting on either side of it. Devon had recovered from the blow to his knee and was now absent-mindedly picking at a zit on his cheek. Doris had resorted to making sexual gestures at Mr. Terminal with her tongues. She began to fondle the snake tongue with a pinky finger. Mr. Terminal swallowed a mouthful of dry air. Doris's pinky finger crawled up her stomach and over one of her breasts, hooked the collar of her shirt and pulled it down, exposing an erect nipple. She smiled a dirty smile. The open newspaper rustled as Mr. and Mrs. Dimplechin, oblivious to their children's antics, argued with one another in angry, inarticulate whispers.

"Excuse me! I have to go to the bathroom!" exclaimed Mr.

Terminal. Nobody responded. Devon shoved a finger up his nose. Doris grabbed her crotch. Mr. Terminal pushed out his lips...and rushed out of the living room. The Dimplechins remained on the couch. Doris threw her head back, opened her mouth and laughed like a dolphin. The other three Dimplechins paid her no mind and went about their questionable business...

There were two long hallways leading out of the living room, one to the right of the couch, one in front of it. Mr. Terminal took the hallway to the right, partly because he was right-handed and Instinct pointed him in that direction, partly because the hallway in front of the couch contained the front door to the Dimplechin's house at its tail end. If he went down there, he might go through the front door and never come back. He was mad at himself for getting so frazzled in the line of fire. But he would pull it together and bounce back. The Dimplechins had turned out to be much more formidable customers than he had expected, but he would turn things around. He just needed to slap himself in the face a few times, talk some trash to his image in the mirror for a few seconds. And maybe take a quick dump.

The hallway was bleached white and there were no paintings hanging on its walls except for one: a painting of a bleached whitewall. The hallway seemed to get smaller as Mr. Terminal staggered down it, looking for the bathroom. Eventually he realized it was in fact getting smaller. By the time he reached the bathroom door, he had to bend his head down to keep it from scraping against the ceiling. "Genius fucking architecture," he mumbled to himself.

"What's that?" said his boss. "What did you say to me?"

Mr. Terminal caught his breath. "Oops. Nothing. Sorry, sir."

His boss cleared a lump of phlegm from his throat. It took

awhile. Then: "Sorry my ass. What're you doing, Terminal?"

"I'm going to the bathroom. I have to use the bathroom."

"Daddy-O & Sonz doesn't pay you to use the bathroom. Are you kidding me? Wise up shithead. Get back out there and sell those bastards a vacuum cleaner. This is serious business here. This is your life, I'm telling you. Don't make me look bad. I have follicles to answer to myself, you know. You act a certain way, you make me look a certain way. Screw this shit up and you'll never walk the streets as a salesman again. That's the truth!"

Mr. Terminal closed his eyes, shook his head. A flashbulb image of an axe slamming into his boss's skull materialized on his mind's screen. He inhaled deeply. "I understand, sir. Don't worry. I won't let you down. Have I ever let you down?"

Lots of dead air before his boss replied. "You have five minutes, Terminal. I'm plugging out. I'm going to get a sandwich. When I get back to my desk and plug back in, you better be kicking ass. Otherwise you're a memory. Do you understand me?"

"I understand, sir," he said. But his boss had already clicked off.

Mr. Terminal closed his eyes again, shook his head again. He liked being a salesman, and he was good at it. But was going through shit like this worth it? He had a degree in haberdashery. He could always quit Daddy-O & Sonz and get a job at a hat store. But selling things in a store was a lot different than selling things door-to-door. Door-to-door sales was for the most part a cold-calling operation that demanded the express use of wit and charm, both of which he had plenty. Store sales, on the other hand, only required a minimal amount of wit and charm, if any at all, since consumers typically don't walk into a store unless they have at least a moderate interest in buying something. Still, it was a consideration—especially if he didn't make good with the Dimplechins. But he would make good with them. He was a warrior, after all. A salesman gladiator. Defeat was not part of his world view.

He opened his eyes. He pushed open the door to the bathroom and walked inside. The door closed behind him, and automatically locked.

It was not a bathroom.

It was...an outhouse?

Instead of the smooth, plaster whitewalls that defined the Dimplechin's hallway, in here were walls made of rotten, stinking wood. And there was no mirror or sink. And no toilet. No porcelain toilet anyway; sitting in the far corner was a cruddy, overturned box with a hole sawed into the top of it. Sticking out of the wall next to it was a roll of crusty wax paper, and decorating the walls were intricate mosaics of piss splatters and shit streaks. The stench was atrocious. Mr. Terminal nearly yakked. But he was too perplexed to yak. Not only by the sordid state of the alleged outhouse, but by what was going on in the alleged outhouse.

There were two men. One was standing up, the other was kneeling down.

The standing man was very old. Had to be in his mid-80s. His bald, scaly head was covered in liver spots, and his hands and arms were covered in bright blue varicose veins. There were also veins all over his gaunt rubicund face, but they were much thinner and didn't stick out. He was wearing a long, black robe that flowered down and out from the tight, leather S&M collar wrapped around his neck. In his fist was a gavel. Apparently the standing man was some kind of judge.

And the kneeling man, apparently, was The Judged.

He was naked, sweaty, grimy. He had paper-thin skin, a rib cage that looked two sizes too big for his dilapidated body. A small swarm of fleas buzzed around the crappy dreadlocks that hung off of his scalp like rotten bananas. In the middle of the dreadlocks was a bald spot, and in the middle of the bald spot was a wound. Blood trickled out of the wound, streamed down the kneeling man's face. It looked like he was wearing a mask of red, dead tapeworms.

Pinching his nose, Mr. Terminal stared at the spectacle of the two men. They didn't stare back. They didn't even acknowledge the sudden intrusion. They carried on with their proceedings as if they were the only two organisms that existed.

"The Law has spoken," intoned the judge, and hammered The Judged on his bald spot with the gavel. The Judged teetered and groaned as blood splashed up into the humid, rank air...

Mr. Terminal made a that's-gotta-hurt face. "What's going on in here?" he said. "Do the Dimplechins know you're in here? What the hell are you two doing?" His pinched nose made his voice sound like a duck's.

The two men made no response. It was as if the vacuum cleaner salesman had said nothing at all. The judge stood there glaring at The Judged with the bulbous eyes of an animé character. The Judged kneeled there, hunch-backed, shivering, sniffling.

"I asked you a question," Mr. Terminal quacked. "I don't know who you are, and I don't care. I'm nobody of consequence. I'm just a salesman. Still, when I ask a question, I expect an answer. What are you doing?"

Slowly the judge turned his heated gaze from the top of The Judged's damaged head to Mr. Terminal's grimacing face. "We are upholding The Law," said the man, "and that is our affair." His gaze remained on Mr. Terminal for a few seconds before returning to its original position. "The Law has spoken," he reiterated, and nailed The Judged again with his gavel. This time The Judged cried out.

Mr. Terminal winced. He had a right mind to walk over to the judge and give him a taste of his own medicine. He refrained, though. The old bat was slight and decrepit-looking, but there was a distinct air of strength about him. Additionally, chances were the Dimplechins knew these two were in here. Maybe they were relatives of the family, delinquent relatives they kept locked away in here, and if he unnerved them, that may not bode well for the sale he had to make. He needed to maintain a certain etiquette no matter how outlandish the situation appeared to be. But that didn't mean he couldn't express his discontent with the apparent situation. He just had to do so in a civilized, respectable manner. And if he played his cards right, maybe, in the end, he could sell these two lunatics a vacuum cleaner. Nothing was impossible, not in his business, and to say the least, this place could use a little tidying up.

Mr. Terminal removed his fingers from his nose. He inhaled. Dry-heaved. Inhaled again. Dry-heaved again. Whisper-swore through clenched teeth...and inhaled again...and dry-heaved again. "Shit!" he said aloud. But he kept at it until his senses had acclimatized to the foul aroma of this in-the-house outhouse and he was able to breathe normally.

He removed two business cards from his coat pocket. His intention was first to politely explain how the judge's treatment of The Judged was perhaps unfair and most definitely less than sophisticated, despite what The Judged was guilty of, and then to give one card to each of them. Then he would explain who he was, why he was here, and how he intended to better their lives by offering them the benefits of a sharp-looking, state-of-the-art, reasonably priced vacuum cleaner.

Just as Mr. Terminal was about to pitch them, there was a knock at the door. "Hello?" said a voice. It was a male voice. A young male's. Devon? Maybe. He couldn't tell. Mr. Terminal held his breath, glanced over at the door out of the corner of his eyes. Waited...

"Is somebody in there?" said another voice. This one belonged to a female. To Doris. "What's the matter in there?"

The judge said, "The Law has spoken." And cracked The Judged where it counted.

"Uhhh," said Mr. Terminal, not knowing what to do, what to say, how to react.

"Open this goddamn door!" screamed a voice that was clearly Mr. Dimplechin's. He was followed by his wife. "Let us in! Let us in there!" The doorknob fidgeted wildly.

All at once the Dimplechins began pounding on the door. As they pounded, they whooped and shrieked as if they were being tortured to death.

"Hold on please!" barked Mr. Terminal. He was sufficiently freaked out at this point. "I'll be out in a second! Please leave me alone for a second!"

They didn't leave him alone. They continued to pound and rant and rave.

"The Law has spoken," said the judge. The Judged threw up and collapsed onto the floor after he was struck with the gavel. The judge said, "Get up! Get up you weird fiend!" Blood was gushing out of his head now. Fleas were buzzing all over the place. He grabbed the judge by the ankles and made inarticulate pleading-for-mercy noises. The

judge kicked him in the face. "Don't touch me!" he wailed. He began
to hop around on his tiptoes, hooting, deranged, furious.

Mr. Terminal slowly backed away. His heart was racing. A
headache, vertigo, nausea was setting in. I'm going to die, he told himself. This is how my life is going to end. I don't deserve this. To die in
this place, with these weirdos. It isn't fair. Nothing's fair in this world.
Life is just a big assfuck. All I want to do is sell a vacuum cleaner. That's
all. Is that too much to ask? I don't think it is. I really don't think it is...

Now Mr. Terminal's boss returned to the scene. "Terminal!" he
shouted, nearly shattering the vacuum cleaner salesman's eardrum.
"You, Terminal! What's all that racket! I'm trying to eat a sandwich!
Fuck's that noise! I can't even think straight over here! Sounds like a
mosh pit over there! What is all that hoo-ha! Answer me bitch!"

He didn't answer him. He had lost the power of speech. He continued to move backwards...until the wall ran into his back, staining it
with feces. He didn't care. He wanted to curl up into a ball and disappear. But he couldn't bend over. He couldn't move.

...The Judged lay on the floor, a pile of naked bones. The judge
stomped on the bones and reduced them to a pool of feverish, steaming
gore. The cacophony of screaming voices outside intensified, it was
pure thunder now, and the door cracked like lightning as the
Dimplechins continued to pulverize it with their fists. The judge
turned to Mr. Terminal. He pointed his finger at him. "This is all your
fault!" he exclaimed. "The court finds you guilty as charged! Prepare
to be punished like the filthy criminal you are!" Crazed, the judge
strode towards Mr. Terminal, his gavel cocked over his gamey head.

Under normal circumstances, Mr. Terminal would have charged
the judge and taken him out with a swift knee to the groin followed by

a frenzy of vicious body blows. But these were not normal circumstances, and Mr. Terminal had reached his wit's end.

Helpless, he calmly opened his mouth. And screamed.

And gasped into consciousness.

He was laying on a thin leather bed in a small white room. He was wearing a cheap grey suit with penny loafers, a striped tie, and pants that were too short for his legs. There was one light bulb hanging down from the middle of the ceiling. On one wall was a large mirror. It looked like a police interrogation room.

It was. But it didn't belong to the police. It belonged to Daddy-O & Sonz. A billboard affixed to one of the room's walls said so:

THIS ROOM IS THE PROPERTY OF

DADDY-O & SONZ

Attached to Mr. Terminal's forehead and face was a web of dermatrodes. He clawed them off in a frenzy. One of the dermatrodes tore his skin when he yanked it. A line of blood flowed down his forehead into his eye. It stung like iodine.

"Christ!" he bleated. He jumped off the bed, got a headrush, almost fainted. Hot, black spots clouded his vision. He shook his head. Licked his cotton-coated lips.

A door opened.

A tall, sinewy man with a giant V-back and an insectlike face stepped into the room. He was wearing a shiny Wickitashi suit and his hair was slicked back. His plastic-looking skin was the color of ocean surf.

Mr. Terminal's vision dove in and out of clarity as the man

approached him. For a moment he blacked out. But he remained standing.

When his vision returned to him, he found himself looking into the eyes of the man.

They stood before each other, staring at each other. One man's stare was icy and calculating, the other's was airy and puzzled. Only a foot or so of empty space separated their bodies.

"Where am I?" said Mr. Terminal, breaking the silence.

"Relax," said the man. He had a raspy, aqueous voice.

Mr. Terminal frowned. "I am relaxed."

The man frowned. "No you are not. I said relax. Do it."

"Where am I?"

"I'm not telling you until you calm down."

"I told you I'm calm," insisted Mr. Terminal.

The man smiled. "No you didn't. You told me you were quote-unquote *relaxed*. See what I mean? You are out of control, sir. Let's just take a moment here, shall we?"

Mr. Terminal was infuriated. He wanted to go. And he had to use the toilet for real now. But if he tried to leave, if he tried to even move from the position he was standing in, he feared he would be annihilated in some way, either by the man standing in front of him, whose physique was much more capable and powerful than his, or by unseen forces—a gang of heavies, possibly, watching him from behind the mirror, waiting for him to make a move. Best stay put. Best wait until things were explained to him. His memory was shot; he couldn't recall anything that had happened before he had talked his way into the Dimplechin's home.

A minute passed. A minute and a half. Two. Mr. Terminal maintained a semi-calm expression on his face. But inside he was a hurricane of anxiety.

Finally the man spoke. "Are you relaxed now?"

Mr. Terminal didn't reply.

"That's more like it," said the man. His breath smelled like olives. "My name is Mr. Yicfung."

"Yicfung? Seriously? What kind of name is that for a person?"

Mr. Yicfung glared at him. "I might ask you the same question, Mr. Terminal."

Mr. Terminal blinked.

Mr. Yicfung rolled his eyes. "Listen to me. Shut your lousy mouth for a second so I can explain things to you. I realize your memory is on hiatus right now. Not to worry. It will return to you in due course. Now then. Are you going to interrupt me all day long or are you going to let me do my job?" He didn't wait for Mr. Terminal to answer. "Right. You are in the corporate offices of Daddy-O & Sonz. This is an interview, and you are an interviewee. What you experienced at the Dimplechin household was a simulation. Those maniacs don't exist, nor does the personal history that was implanted into your virtual self. You have not been with this firm for over ten years. This is the first time you have ever been here, and you're here because you want a job. Fifteen minutes ago you walked into my office. We shook hands, firmly, but not too firmly. We bullshitted for a few minutes about trivial alpha male bullshit. You informed me about your personal and professional past. Finally you signed a document and subjected yourself to the aforementioned simulation, the purpose of which was to test your endurance as a potential vacuum cleaner salesman for this firm. The circumstances under which you were tested were purposely outlandish—but not outlandish to the point of being altogether unreal. It gets weird out there in the field sometimes, Mr. Terminal, and we here at Daddy-O want to know what kind of man will be representing us when the heat is on. Are you following me so far? Nod if you are." He didn't wait for Mr. Terminal to nod. "Right. In addition to your actions and words, your thoughts were also monitored. We witnessed everything that passed through your head as the goings-on of the simulation increased in intensity. Generally speaking, Mr. Terminal, you are a sick pervert. The dirty things you thought! Do you moonlight as a porno actor, I wonder? Every few seconds, it seemed, some kind of x-rated image flashed onto your mind's screen. But that is of no consequence. Your sexual mania is not what interests us. What interests us is the way in which you, as a sales-man and a Daddy-O rep, dealt with the oppressive forces that were working against you. Did you maintain an always-be-closing attitude? How often did you experience moments of helplessness and weakness? Did you show mental respect for your superior? Were you at all times prepared to lie, manipulate, and cheat your way to a sale? Did you at any time badmouth Daddy-O & Sonz? When we screen interviewees like yourself, these are the types of questions we ask ourselves."

Mr. Yicfung paused. He was still standing face-to-face with Mr. Terminal, whose memory was slowly leaking back into him. "I'm beginning to remember," he said.

"I know you are," snapped Mr. Yicfung. He angrily spit on the floor. "I didn't lie to you when I said you would regain your memory. Are you calling me a liar? I think you are."

Mr. Terminal could no longer resist fighting back, despite the possible consequences. He remembered now that he had been laid off by his former employer, a small, independently owned vacuum cleaner company that had been forced to declare bankruptcy. He wasn't married and didn't have any children to support, but he did own a relatively expensive apartment. There were bills to pay. He needed this job. At the same time, he was nobody's bitch. Mr. Yicfung was treating him like a piece of shit. He could no longer tolerate it. He had to say something. "Why are you being so góddamn snotty with me?" he said. "I've been very polite and respectful to you. Is this a test, too? Are you trying to get me to lose my temper?"

"Everything in life is a test," replied Mr. Yicfung, "but that is neither here nor there."

Mr. Terminal squinted in confusion. "Excuse me? I don't know what that means."

"Then you should probably keep your assumptions and your questions to yourself, shouldn't you."

"Perhaps."

"Perhaps? Perhaps you better not say perhaps anymore."

"Why not?"

"That's for me to know and for you to not find out."

"Pardon me for saying so, but that's not a very mature thing to say, Mr. Yicfung."

"What do you know about maturity, Mr. Terminal?"

"I know enough to know we're standing here staring at and talking to each other like a couple of clowns."

"That's your opinion. Nothing more, nothing less."

Mr. Terminal's hands curled into tight fists. "This is stupid."

"What is stupid? I don't know what the word *this* refers to. The sentence that just came out of your mouth doesn't make *this* clear."

"Can you just tell me if I got the job or not? Given your acidic tone, I'm assuming I didn't."

"To make an assumption is to entertain chaos. Don't do it. I'm warning you."

"All I want to know is if I got the job."

"All I want to know is why that is all you want to know."

Mr. Yicfung chewed his lip, awaiting a response. He didn't get one. Mr. Terminal realized he should have kept his mouth shut. He couldn't get a straight answer out of Mr. Yicfung unless he allowed the man to speak of his own free will. If he kept on speaking to him, they would be here all day and night, talking in circles. If Mr. Terminal wanted answers, he would have to play Mr. Yicfung's stupid game.

"I'm going to button my lips now," said Mr. Terminal, and buttoned his lips.

They stared at each other.

And stared at each other. The expression on Mr. Yicfung's white, tensile face was as inexpressive as the expression on Mr. Terminal's flushed, aquiline face.

At last Mr. Yicfung resumed his monologue as if he had never been interrupted. "On the whole you tested below average. You showed virtually no mental respect to your superior, and while you experienced moments of positivity and conviction, your outlook was for the most part negative and worrisome. At one point you swallowed in distress. At another you accused life of being a quote-unquote *big assfuck*. These are not the mental actions of a strong person. You may think you are a strong person, but you are not. You are weak and insecure. The fact that you ran away from the Dimplechins like a little girl when Doris pulled out her nipple and showed it to you is additional proof of this sad fact. A real man would have capitalized on that nipple. A real man would have devised some means of coming to terms with the nipple without causing a scene. And we here at Daddy-O & Sonz like real men." Mr. Yicfung paused again. Mr. Terminal was a hair's breadth away from punching him in the nose. He was a reasonable follicle, but the blow his manhood had just sustained was beyond reason. If Mr. Yicfung said one more bad thing about him, there was no way he would be able to contain himself.

Mr. Yicfung smirked. "That said," he continued, "the firm was particularly impressed by one aspect of your performance, so much so that we are willing to overlook your utter lack of machismo. I'm talking about your intention to sell the two men in the bathroom a vacuum cleaner despite the absurdist nature of that situation. You didn't follow through with this intention, of course. You cracked before you could. But everybody who has endured the simulation has cracked. Even me. What is important to us is that you had the notion to sell a vacuum cleaner to two seemingly fucked up wackos who, to say the least, possessed neither the means nor the inclination to purchase a vacuum cleaner. Not only that, at one point, immediately after you called life an assfuck, you thought to yourself, and I quote, 'All I want to do is sell a vacuum cleaner.' Amazing. Brilliant. Outstanding. Usually when a man thinks he's standing in front of death's door, he prays to God, or he thinks about loved ones, or he thinks about having sex with a celebrity. But not you. You thought about selling a vacuum cleaner. No interviewee has ever done something like that before. In this respect you are truly one of a kind. In this respect you are truly Daddy-O & Sonz material. The board members all agree." He used a thumb to point over his shoulder at the mirror. "You are the one, Mr. Terminal.

Today is your lucky day. You may be a pretty boy, but we believe that you have the capacity to make us a lot of money. And money, of course, is far more important to us than you being a pretty boy. Welcome to the show."

Mr. Yicfung stuck out his hand.

Mr. Terminal studied the hand. Hairless and perfectly smooth, it looked like a prosthetic. Part of him wanted to shake it, part of him wanted to tell Mr. Yicfung what he thought of him and then beat the shit out of him.

He grasped the hand. Shook it.

"Well done, sir," said Mr. Yicfung, shaking back. "Well done indeed. In spite of your shortcomings, I believe you are a capable man. And now if you wouldn't mind removing your clothes and kneeling down please."

Mr. Terminal made a constipated face. "What?" he said.

"You heard me," said Mr. Yicfung, loosening his hand from Mr. Terminal's grip. He took hold of one of his ears.

"What are you doing?" Mr. Terminal asked.

Mr. Yicfung's answer was a small, crooked smile.

He yanked his ear.

He ripped his face off in one swift motion...and revealed the face of...

As Mr. Terminal cried out and began to back into a corner, the walls of the clean white room quickly metamorphosed into the walls of a reeking, crap-stained outhouse. "What is this!" he shouted, falling into a cowering position on the floor. "What are you!"

The judge removed a gavel from his suit coat, which metamorphosed into a long black robe. "This is nothing," he breathed, "and I am something." He flowed over to the corner like a ghost, loomed over

The Judged with hellish resolve. Flakes of dead, wet skin drizzled off of his bald head like sleet. "Don't make me take off your clothes for you," he said.

"Leave me alone! Let me go!"

"I can't do that," the judge whispered. "I *won't* do that."

"Why not!" Mr. Terminal growled through clenched teeth.

The judge raised the gavel over his head. He widened his eyes. He pursed his lips. He nodded gravely.

He said, "Because The Law has spoken."

Behind the mirror, the Dimplechins leapt out of their chairs and began to breakdance...

The Stick Figure

A stick figure crawled out of a manhole. It was nine feet tall and wore a pelt of smooth obsidian skin over its long pencil-thin extremities. Its head was perfectly round and black and lacked hair, ears, eyeballs, and a nose. There was a mouth, however—a gaping hole it used to murder a passing flâneur.

The flâneur was caught entirely off guard. He had mistaken the stick figure for a lamppost, an object he took pride in ignoring, and was in no position to defend himself when his head was bitten off and then spit out like a pinch of tobacco.

The head knit its brow as it tumbled across the street and vanished into a sewer with its fedora intact. A few innocent bystanders watched the head go with idle curiosity.

"Momma didn't love me," the stick figure said to the bystanders, and screamed.

The bystanders screamed back. They felt badly for the stick figure: on top of being the only one of its kind and allegedly not being loved by at least one of its parents, it was the only one screaming. They felt obliged to keep it company.

The stick figure misinterpreted the counter-scream as a fearsome reaction to the murder of the flâneur. It stopped screaming. The bystanders followed suit. Confused, the stick figure pushed out its lips, recollecting the dead...flashbulb of mnemonic imagery...It had not always been this way. There was a time when it had a real life. A job, a family, infinite debt. Then one day it was walking down the street and somebody shouted, "Hey, he's just a big stick figure!"...The gig was up. The stick figure retreated to the sewers, surfacing only to allay its loneliness and externalize its pent-up aggression by means of manhandling and annihilating strangers. On occasion it liked to purchase a deli sandwich, too.

"Are you all right?" asked one of the bystanders. Like the others, he was wearing a bystander uniform: fighter pilot hat, oversized mirrorshades, handlebar mustache, press-on chin, trench coat, construction boots...

The stick figure snapped out of his reverie. "I'm fine," it replied, and attacked.

Continuing to empathize with it, the bystanders allowed it to attack. They stood there calmly, listlessly, with compassionate expressions on their faces as the stick figure lashed out at them with its sharp limbs, tearing off appendages and heads with the fervor of an excited child tearing wrapping paper off of its Christmas presents. It was a gruesome spectacle. Hot gore littered the streets in every direction. Still, the bystanders were undaunted. Their empathy for the estranged stick figure surmounted their fear of it, and they continued to stand firm and tall, patiently waiting to die painful, ultraviolent deaths.

Word spread quickly about the stick figure's killing spree. The technology of the media was such that in a few moments time the entire city knew about it. PCP flowed out of skyscrapers and alleyways and gathered on the sidewalks and streets, rendering Pseudofollic-ulitis City a virtual receptacle of innocent bystanders willing to give up their lives for the sake of the stick figure's degradation.

But the stick figure was not a monster. Not metaphorically, at least. It hadn't slaughtered two block's worth of bystanders before it started to feel guilty about its actions, wishing it could take them back. It was strangling two men, one in each hand, when Guilt sunk in its teeth. Both men were blank-faced, displaying no visible discomfort or pain despite the dark purple tint of their skin. When they were abruptly released, however, they massaged their Adam's apples and took small gulps of air. The stick figure sat down on a curb and buried in its hands the great bowling ball that was its head.

"I'm sorry," it whispered.

A bystander who was within reach of the whisper whispered back, "Don't worry about it. We all have our dog days."

The media immediately spread word that the stick figure had calmed down. PCP sighed, checked their watches, and moped back into their respective spacescrapers and alleyways. If they happened to pass the crouching stick figure on their way, they gave it a pat on the back or a piece of optimistic advice. The gestures made it feel worse. By the time the streets were empty (except for the odd group of bystanders, of course), it was curled up on its side in a fetal position.

The stick figure fell asleep and had a dream about a stick figure who dreamed it was a bystander. The dream didn't last long. When it was over the stick figure woke up, sat up, stretched, stood up, and yawned.

Before disappearing into a manhole, the stick figure stopped by a deli to purchase a ham and cheese on rye...

Horoscope

The following horoscope was originally published in *The Horseshit Herald* on the forty-ninth day of Pseudober in the year of our Founder 11,966 A.T.F. Since then it has been reprinted in various forms in hundreds of thousands of newspapers (including *The Horseshit Herald* itself) as well as in magazines, comic books, plaquedemic journals, phonebooks, cookbooks, underground propaganda leaflets, Bibles, coffee table assembly instructions, sandwich wrappers, and other noteworthy publications.

Aries

Happy days and delicious nights are on the horizon for you. Unfortunately a desert of vast eternity lies between you and the horizon. As an Aries, you enjoy challenges and take pleasure in dominating PCP, but this month your pleasure-principle will be tested. Expect to be violated in some capacity by a close friend or relative. Ready yourself for a persistent stream of hate mail sent to you by strangers for no apparent reason. Be prepared to fall in love with a lion tamer who assures you she loves you and then has anal sex with your best friend in your front yard while the whole neighborhood is watching.

Make sure you are fit to go bankrupt and possibly to lose a limb in a freak unicycling accident. Stay clear of Virgos and Capricorns: one will try to take advantage of you in a financial matter, the other will try to goose you when you least expect it. You are inclined to be generous and forthright, but you would do well to resist your inclinations, adopting an unapologetic narcissistic attitude and talking as much shit as possible. Do not underestimate heavy-breathing bogeymen hiding underneath your bed. Do not underestimate boogie dancers either.

Virgo

Despite being antagonized by the occasional altruistic impulse, you are a loser, a moron, and a ninny. Your neuroses are dark and deep-seated, rendering you as ugly on the inside as on the outside. You smell, even though you are a chronic shower taker. You have halitosis and a brown smile, even though you are a manic tooth brusher. The one redeeming quality in your repertoire is that you do not have a hairy back; otherwise you are distasteful in virtually every imaginable way. You will undoubtedly be ridiculed and beaten up this month by at least four strangers who find you offensive-looking. Your hairline will also recede another half inch, assuming you have any hair left. Your inexcusable monobrow is inexcusably bushy. Your love handles are out of control. As always, no romantic interludes lay in wait for you in the near future. Stay away from fire hydrants, low-fat yogurt, and circus folk on stilts. And remember: any attempt to improve upon yourself will only exacerbate your always-already ignominious condition.

Taurus

The world may be your oyster, but your oyster is a rotten bastard:

instead of a pearl its tongue contains a large rabbit pellet. It has a dirty mouth, too, literally and figuratively—not only does it hurl obscenities at random passersby for no reason at all, its once full-figured lips have corroded into slobbery brown lobes, the result of years of unbridled cigar smoking and tobacco chewing. There is no excuse for your oyster. Yet you persist in thinking that it is ideal. Your world view is despicable in this fashion. Do us PCP a favor and flush your oyster down the toilet, or at least steam-cook it and wash it down with a nice glass of sauvignon blanc. Avoid asparagus.

Gemini

There is an ominous wart on your nose that induces disgusted double-takes from children and PCP who lack the social skills and resolution to pretend that the wart does not exist. There are chins all over your neck. Who could ever desire the likes of you? There are liver spots all over your extremities. There is a chip on your shoulder the size of The Abyss. There is a doppelgänger reeking havoc in the waiting room of your mind. Your homeliness is hypnotic. Your emotional disposition is a dystopia. Rumor has it that Geminis are charming and that their existence makes life a better, more beautiful place to be. This rumor was started by a Scorpio named Hans "Deterritorialized Flow" Hossenfeffer who developed a distaste for a Gemini named Petunia "Machinic Assemblage" Easyjapanesey. The jezebel cheated on him with a Leo named Clyde "BwO (Body without Organs)" Noreaster. So "Deterritorialized Flow" and his cronies started telling everybody in town that Geminis were nice and attractive and happy-go-lucky. As a result, everybody sought out the Geminis in hopes that their good qualities would rub off on them, and when they discovered the abominable condition of the Geminis, they hated them all the more. (In the end, many of the Geminis were ostracized from the city. A few were beaten and tortured to death. "Machinic Assemblage," for instance, was stoned and disemboweled in Willynilly Square.) The point is, you are a coxcomb in need of a good old-fashioned suggulation followed by a defenestration. Dark fairy tales will be written about you based on your looks alone (although as you and I both know one's image produces one's personality). You're broken, and all the King's horses and all the King's men and the court jesters and scops and damsels in distress and street urchins can't put you back together again.

Cancer

As your zodiac sign plainly suggests, you are a cancer to society, contributing nothing worthwhile to the daily operations of the human race. It's time to stop letting your emotions control your life. You walk around all day laughing, and crying, and being passionate, and losing your temper, and gesticulating, and telling jokes and horror stories, and slapping PCP on the back, and trying to hug strangers and estranged lovers and would-be family members...Everybody's had enough of your melodramatic baloney. Try internalizing yourself, for the love of God. Stand in front of the mirror and practice maintaining a blank expression for at least one hour every morning until you are able to socialize in the public sphere like a semi-functional human being. This month the urge to write and publish a memoir will overpower you. Fight this urge—your life experiences are as boring and plain as your smile. The ennui that distinguishes your inner self is the very reason you take such reckless delight in the hideous process of externalization. Why is it so difficult for you to get past yourself? Why do you insist on carrying on conversation after conversation during which you blab and blather about yourself without one moment's concern for the feelings, insights, and convictions of your interlocutors? Listen for once: you might learn a thing or two. You would do well to place a square of duct tape over your mouth. Better yet, staple your mouth shut. The pain you feel may help to sublimate the desire to inflict yourself on innocent bystanders who want nothing more than to mind their own business.

Libra

Etc. Etc.

Leo

Leo. You know what you are. Everybody knows. No need to repeat it here. The same thing will befall you this month that befell you last month. That is what happens when you are a son of a bitch and your sense of self-importance is so large it is required by The Law to have a driver's license, a social security number, and a NO TRESPASSING sign affixed to its great and terrible bulk. If I were you, I would very likely take my own life. If you are too cowardly to take your own life, I would at least slap myself around a little. Or you might invite me over to your house to slap you around. We could drink apértifs and eat dinner first. Please plan accordingly. For the record, I prefer red meat to white meat, I detest vegetables and fruits, and I will not tolerate being served a meal without subsequently being served a desert, preferably key lime pie. Accompanying this pie should be a hand-somely poured Manhattan in a snifter glass and a Cuban cigar the size of your forearm. Thank you in advance, sir...

Scorpio

"No matter where you go, no matter what you touch, there is cancer and syphilis. It is written in the sky; it flames and dances, like an evil portent. It has eaten into our souls and we are nothing but a dead thing like the moon." This excerpt from Henry Miller's *Tropic of Cancer* speaks directly to your condition. Your degradation is precisely why you are preoccupied with issues of self-mastery and power as a means of compensation for that which you lack. The same goes for your so-called psychic abilities: you have come to believe that you can read minds, diagnose strange illnesses, and shoot beams of static electricity out of your fingertips because you know very well how inadequate you are as a social subject. Do you know what I would do to you if you tried to shoot a beam of static electricity out of your fingertip at me? I would drape you over my knee and spank you like a little child! Watch out for *infra dig* barbermongers.

Sagittarius

Your undying hunger for knowledge will lead you past dark alleyways in the near future. These alleyways will call out to you, taunting you, calling you names, begging you to walk down them. I would advise you not to listen to them. Listen to me instead. Your impulsiveness and insatiable curiosity, however, will of course compel you not to listen to me. But you should listen to me. I'm just trying to help you by pointing out the variables of your character. It's absolutely amazing how little PCP know about themselves. This is because PCP lack perception. Or they choose not to exercise perception. Or they are ridiculous dumb-asses. My apologies if this hard truth offends you. I'm simply laying things on the table *au naturel*. There is absolutely no reason to ignore me, no reason not to heed my warning. I don't write horoscopes for my health. Granted, I sprinkle a healthy pinch of horseshit on each entry. At the same time, each entry is grounded in something like the truth. I only ask that you make an effort to do as I say. Is that too much to ask? I don't think so, I don't think so...

Aquarius

It's not an easy thing to be me. Always writing down the bones of other PCP. Other PCP's emotional spectrums, other PCP's love interests, other PCP's tastes, desires, stupidities, inhibitions. Being a horoscope writer is a selfless business, and in today's post-real age, it is extremely difficult to be selfless. But what about me? I'm not a completely uninteresting character. I possess a certain amount of wit and international intrigue. When I write and publish my memoirs, readers will at least raise an eyebrow here and there. In all likelihood their eyebrows will raise so frequently and with such gusto that their foreheads will go numb and they will have to resort to making surprised noises with their mouths and nonplussed yet fascinated huffs with their nostrils. Considering their fervent desire to sponge up knowledge and seek out the truth, Aquariuses especially will find my memoirs to their liking. Pisces may be piqued as well, if for nothing else than the fact that I am a Pisces and, by reading me, you will no doubt learn all you need to know about yourself and more...

Capricorn

I like to have a drink until I am absolutely shitfaced when I finish writing for the day. My drink of choice is Petron tequila. I like to have it poured into a highball glass and to sip it delicately, savorily, as if it might be the cup of hot black morning coffee I drink every day to assist in the warding off of each morning's hangover. This sipping business lasts for about two drinks. Then I begin to wolf down glasses of Petron, shooting them back to back. Capricorns may find themselves engaging in a similar ritual in order to spruce up the monotony of the boring lives they lead. You may also drink a lot because your unconscious is making an effort to express your inner satyr (remember, the original Greek derivation of Capricorn is "goat-horned"). I have never actually seen a drunk Capricorn. I have seen a number of drunk PCP before, but I did not ask any of them to identify their sign at risk of sounding as if I was either trying to pick them up or sell them something. But I don't need to ask PCP to identify their signs for me. All I need is half a minute to study their public demeanor and behavior and I know what they are. Capricorns are especially easy to recognize. They are the goody-goody-two-shoes of society and they always wear their just intentions on their faces. They are also the ones who repeatedly employ the exclamation "Lansakes!" whenever they are asked about their well-being. Example: "How are you doing today?" "Lansakes! I'm doing fine." The communal use of this word by Capricorns is an utter mystery to me as it is clearly not a cultural formation—Capricorns are available for existence in all sizes, shapes and colors—and we can be fairly certain that all of the world's Capricorns did not get together at some point for a secret meeting in order to discuss, for whatever reason, the perpetuation of the word's use among their kind. It annoys me, Lansakes. If it were up to me, I would have the word struck from the human lexicon. Other words I would strike include *indeed, pejorative, contradistinction, discalceate, utilize, oftentimes, ergo*, *shall*, *palimpsest*, *umbriferous*, *doodad*, and *whippersnapper*, all of which are either out of date, fancy words PCP supplement for simple words to make themselves sound intelligent, or words whose meaning is too difficult for my mnemonic facilities to retain.

Pisces

How will I begin my memoirs? I've often deliberated the question. The question has induced insomnia in me on more than a few occasions. And when I fall asleep, it gives me nightmares. Perhaps I should begin like Jean-Jacques Rousseau, who in *The Confessions* writes, "I have resolved on an enterprise which has no precedent, and which, once complete, will have no imitator. My purpose is to display to my kind a portrait in every way true to nature, and the man I shall portray will be myself." Or perhaps I should begin like John Jacob Jingleheimer Rabinowitz a.k.a. The Founder, who in *Chronicles of a Fucking Asshole* writes, simply, "I am a fucking asshole." I think either introduction would be sufficient. Then again, something altogether different and unique to my personal experience might better suit me. For example: "I was born, I was discarded in a sewer, I was found and raised by a society of mutated alligators who treated me as one of their own. Later, when I realized I was a man, I crawled out of a manhole and asked a passerby to direct me to the nearest sandwich dispenser." But I have difficulty finding the words to adequately express the truth about my life and selfhood. Do words even possess the power to express the truth? Civilized communication, after all, amounts to nothing more than the conveyance of a series of word combinations that exhibit so-called meaning. Removing a word, or replacing one, or relocating it elsewhere can result in semantic catastrophe, not to mention that meaning itself is a subjective business. One series of word combinations might mean one thing to one PCP and another thing to another PCP. It's really all just a bunch of hoo-ha, if you ask me. But I don't suspect you will ask me. Nobody asks me anything. That's why I became a horoscope writer: I get to tell PCP things about themselves and the world whether they like it or not. True, I have no medical insurance, but I am paid handsomely enough that, if something nasty were to happen to me, I could afford to hire a good euthanasist. I almost wish something nasty would happen to me so that I would have an excuse to hire a euthanasist. I am not afraid to die. Death does not frighten me. What frightens me—is life.

Ah yes. *There* is my beginning...

About the Author

D. Harlan Wilson has published over 100 stories in magazines, journals and anthologies throughout the world. He is the author of *The Kafka Effekt, Irrealities* and *Stranger on the Loose.* Currently he skulks around the depths of lower Michigan teaching college writing and literature. For more information on Wilson and his work, visit his official website at www.dharlanwilson.com.

Spider Pie
by Alyssa Sturgill,
104 pgs

Sturgill's debut book firmly establishes her as the *enfant terrible* of contemporary surrealism. Laden with gothic horror sensibilities, it's a one-way trip down a rabbit hole inhabited by sexual deviants and monsters, fairytale beginnings and hideous endings. Includes an introduction by D. Harlan WIlson and is heavily illustrated.

Last Burn in Hell by John Edward Lawson, 150 pgs

Kenrick Brimley is the state prison's official gigolo. From his romance with serial arsonist Leena Manasseh to his lurid angst-affair with a lesbian music diva, from his ascendance as unlikely pop icon to otherwordly encounters, the one constant truth is that he's got no clue what he's doing. As unrelenting as it is original, *Last Burn in Hell* is John Edward Lawson at his most scorching intensity, serving up sexy satire and postmodern pulp with his trademark day-glow prose.

Tempting Disaster editor John Edward Lawson, 260 pgs

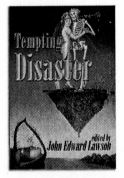

An anthology from the fringe that examines our culture's obsession with sexual taboos. Postmodernists and surrealists band together with renegade horror and sci-fi authors to re-envision what is "erotic" and what is "acceptable." By turns humorous and horrific, shocking and alluring, the authors dissect those impulses we deny in our daily lives. Includes stories by Carlton Mellick III, Michael Hemmingson, Lance Olsen & Jeffrey Thomas.

The Fall of Never by Ronald Damien Malfi, 347 pgs

A young woman, long estranged from her family, is forced to return home when her sister is involved in a mysterious accident. After years of suppressing the past she must struggle to remember for her sister's sake. But nothing is as it seems in Spires, her ancestral home, where cold hearts rule the hearth and deadly secrets lurk in the forest. Plunged back into the dream-world of her youth Kelly is faced with the reality of her own role in the tragedies afflicting her family.

Play Dead by Michael A. Arnzen, 272 pgs

Johnny had given up cards for good until he stumbled onto a different game. A game where you have to make the cards before you play them and the stakes are the highest he's ever seen. When the payout is survival and folding means death the question becomes: are you playing the cards or are they playing you? Using 52 chapters Arnzen's novel-of-cards is stacked with mischief and thrills. Like the most accomplished blackjack dealer Arnzen will keep you guessing at his hand.

100 Jolts by Michael A. Arnzen, 156 pgs

This collection features 100 short shots of fiction guaranteed to stun. From his hilarious satire on technical manuals, "Stabbing for Dummies," to his series of "Skull Fragments" vignettes Arnzen proves he has honed his craft to deliver the highest voltage using the fewest words. "100 Jolts delivers far more than is promised by its title; with this magnificent collection of literate and disturbing short-shorts, some which are among the darkly funniest I've ever read." —Gary A. Braunbeck

Fugue XXIX by Forrest Aguirre

Fugue XXIX is the first collection available from World Fantasy Award winning editor and author Forrest Aguirre. These tales come to you from the fringe of speculative lierary fiction where innovative minds keep busy dreaming up the future's uncharted territories and mining fogotten treasures of the past. Anything can happen, and does, with surprising regularity.

Westermead by Scott Thomas, 292 pgs

Ways of old merge with the magical in this wondrous world. Experience Westermead's thaw and awakening season by season, the lush heat of summer's passion and the retreat into winter's desolate embrace. Come celebrate and mourn with the people of Westermead as they make their way through a world steeped in beauty and dread. With storytelling this vibrant, it's easy to get lost in Thomas' unique landscape.

Printed in the United States
39841LVS00015B/1-30